Praise

A J Dalton's writing

'Unique ideas and a story that develops in an unpredictable manner.' - Fantasy-Faction.com

'Gives you an interesting setting and a devilishly good villain.' - SFX

'Engaging, filled with sacrifice, adventure and some very bloody battles!' - SciFi Now magazine

'The best young British fantasy author on the circuit at the moment.' - Waterstones central buyer

'Very, very clever and manages to offer something different over the traditional fantasy fare. Different, fresh and unique.' - Sfbook.com

'With its rich tapestry of characters and incident there is never a dull moment.'
- FantasyBookReview.co.uk

'There's interesting world building to discover and a surprising amount of dry humour to enjoy. A great deal of fun and certainly worthy of your time!'- The Eloquent Page

'A. J. Dalton's world building is fresh with new ideas.' - IWillReadBooks.com

'Fast moving and keeps you gripped at all times, while also creating a world with immense depth and complexity. Five stars!'- Amazon Review

'A J Dalton, thank you, what I've read will stay with me for a long time.'- *GoodReads.com.*

'Adam Dalton in particular is a discovered Master of Fantasy...read and let the words take you down the rabbit hole!' - Amazon Review

'Dalton's characters are complex and he has ways of twisting events and viewpoints that will often surprise me (in a good way!)! Politics, mythology and magic are woven into the fabric of the story creating a rich tapestry.' - Amazon Review

The Book
of Witches

A J Dalton

kristell-ink.com

Here be witches! by A J Dalton © 2020
The House in Brooklyn by Nadine Dalton-West © 2020
Greenford by Adam Lively © 2020
At The Witching Hour by Isabella Hunter © 2020
The Witch of Soneton by A J Dalton © 2020
In the Shadow of Pendle by Garry Coulthard © 2020
Wytchfynder by Michael Conroy © 2020
Heart's Desire by Michael Victor Bowman © 2020
Three Conversations or How I Burned your Mother by Matt Beeson © 2020

ISBN 978-1-913562-10-6 (Hardback)
ISBN 978-1-913562-11-3 (Paperback)
ISBN 978-1-913562-12-0 (EPUB)

Cover art by Charlotte Pang
Cover design by Ken Dawson
Typesetting by Book Polishers

Kristell Ink

An Imprint of Grimbold Books

5 St John's Way,
Hempton,
Oxfordshire,
OX15 0QR
United Kingdom

www.kristell-ink.com

Dedicated to every woman or person who has suffered persecution or demonization for who they are.

Contents

An Introduction: Here Be Witches!

The Witch of Endor who appears in the Bible is far from being a negative character. Indeed, she helps the character of Saul, the first King of Israel, commune with the spirit of the deceased prophet Samuel. The witch is frightened at the sound of Samuel's voice, and Saul is terrified when the ghost berates him for disobeying God, and when the ghost repeats an earlier prophecy that Saul and his entire army will perish on the battlefield the next day. Seeing Saul's distress, the witch comforts him and provides him with nourishment before he leaves.

For all her necromancy and divining magicks, there is no explicit condemnation of the Witch of Endor in the Bible, she is never presented as malign, and the plot of the story goes on to punish Saul rather than her. She is certainly not described as a wicked, warty, hook-nosed woman who wears a conical black hat, rides a broomstick and has a black cat for a familiar.

We might wonder, then, where and when women, female power or female witches were first properly demonised. Unsurprisingly, it occurs when the sex-act itself (the act which fully exposes female gender, attraction and potential empowerment) becomes more demonised within Western European culture, when the sinful nature of sex is reaffirmed as a defining aspect of Christian doctrine, policy, behaviour,

3

judgement and censure. It was in the Middle Ages that celibacy among Catholic priests truly became widespread, none of the Popes between 1003AD and 1265AD being married, unlike in the periods preceding and following. This ideological assertion allowed the Church to exercise an even greater controlling power over the individual: for sexual instinct, personal desire and even private thoughts and actions were placed (via confession) within a framework of moral, social and legal judgement; and sexual congress could only take place within the Church-controlled sacrament of marriage. More than that, our very bodies and minds (in being desirous of the sexual act) were made sinful, or sin-made-flesh, and in need of the ministrations of the Church. Thereby, Satan became even more real, because he was in us and a part of us. Sexual desire became his tempting words in our minds and the sexual act became him possessing our bodies. Hence, we have the tradition that he could only be cast out by a flagellation of the flesh or an exorcism performed by a priest.

Through this demonising of sex (sexual corruption), the committing of 'original sin' was no longer Adam and Eve simply stealing the forbidden fruit of knowledge: now it was Eve seducing Adam with sexual knowledge of a penile snake; and their shame no longer concerned the theft, but rather concerned their nakedness. Through this demonization of sex, the 'fall' of man (and the Roman empire) during the pre-Christian era was now perceived as being synonymous with a time of Roman orgies, sexual decadence and festivals (like the Saturnalia) dedicated to pagan gods (like Venus, Bacchus and Pan) who were celebrated and worshipped via acts of sexual depravity and promiscuity.

Unfortunately, it was also through this demonization of sex that, as per a homo- or heteronormative patriarchy, as per Eve's seduction of Adam, women and female sexuality became particular agents and an agency of Satan. Thus, the concept of the *succubus* (female demon) was born. According to the Zohar, a foundational work of Jewish mystical thought, which first appeared in thirteenth century Spain, published by the Jewish writer Moses de Leon, Adam's first wife was Lilith, and she left the Garden of Eden to mate with the archangel Samael (read as Satan) and to be transformed into a succubus and queen of demons.

The folk tradition that arose around Lilith in the early Middle Ages has only continued to grow. Her main two aspects are i) the demonic succubus who, jealous of Adam and all those existing happily within the holy sacrament of marriage, only seeks to seduce married men and lead them into sin and damnation ii) the witch who comes at night ('night hag') to strangle innocent children, and so lead their parents into inconsolable despair and damnation. Here, then, is the first 'wicked witch': she who lives outside the norms of society, who has no loving husband or family of her own, and whose entire intent is the destruction of all God-fearing communities. This creature lives at the edges of society (in dark woods, for example) and has access to arcane or magical knowledge that the Church does not possess, and which the Church therefore forbids to others lest the supremacy of God's Church in the world be subverted.

We can understand from all of the above that the Church of the Middle Ages onwards explicitly laid claim to authority over the individual's heart and soul (body and mind) and, as a patriarchal institution, implicitly marginalised female power. Any woman engaged in a spiritual, ritualistic or pseudo-scientific practice which did not operate within or *submit to* the Church's social, moral, religious and educational ideological framework of patriarchal power and authority would be branded a witch, marginalised and potentially executed by ducking or burning. As a result, mid-wives (who might have medical knowledge beyond the Church), older spinsters (who might have independent wealth), herb-women (who definitely had medical knowledge beyond the Church), grandmothers and female elders (who might have the oral history, knowledge, experience and personal influence to threaten patriarchal power) and single women in general were subject to suspicion, close scrutiny and false accusation the length and breadth of the UK, and across Europe.

It was when the Church's relationship with the state (monarchy) began to change that the definition and accusation of witchcraft also changed, becoming politicized and a more overt political weapon. Under the rule of Henry VIII, the Act of Supremacy was passed in 1534, seeing the UK split from the Catholic Church in Rome, thereby laying the foundations for the Church of England. Henry then made a grab for the wealth and power of the Catholic Church in the UK, overseeing the Dissolution of the Monasteries 1536-41, that then enabling him to better fund his overseas military campaigns. In 1542, the UK's first Witchcraft Act was passed, defining witchcraft as a crime for the first time, a crime that was always punishable by death and, significantly, also by the confiscation of the criminal's entire wealth. If the actual text of the Witchcraft Act of 1542 is examined, it is clear that the act is a further move against the Catholic Church in the UK, for it criminalises any and all religious, spiritual or ritualistic practice that involves an invocation of spirits (such as Catholic saints), particularly when that which is 'devysed, practised or exercised' leads the individual to 'fynde money or treasure […] for lucre of money' or 'goodes stolen or lost'. Importantly, this was the moment when the possibility of *male witches* was understood, recognised and defined.

The Witchcraft Act of 1542 only lasted until 1547, when

Henry died and the act was repealed. It was not replaced until the Witchcraft Act of 1563 ('An Act Against Conjurations, Enchantments and Witchcrafts') under Elizabeth I (1558-1603). Elizabeth's Witchcraft Act was in some ways more merciful than Henry's, for it only demanded a death sentence for witchcraft that had led to the death of another; otherwise, the witchcraft only resulted in imprisonment. Elizabeth required a law that would allow her to censure (Catholic) religious or spiritual practice if she chose, but that would also allow a certain leniency if she wished to avoid unduly antagonising Catholics in England and the great Catholic states of Europe (France, Spain and Italy). Elizabeth, of course, had similarly used the possibility of her marrying a foreign (Catholic) king to negotiate, mollify and pacify the threat from Europe. As with Henry before her, however, the concept of the witch was politicized, a political tool and, as necessary, a political weapon. When it suited her, Elizabeth would tolerate witchcraft, notoriously permitting herself a court magician in the person of John Dee, who practised necromancy with an obsidian mirror in which he could conjure the spirits of the dead. Yet when the threat from Europe became too great (as with the Spanish Armada in 1588), Elizabeth would conduct purges of Catholics under the auspices of her Witchcraft Act of 1563. It was also in 1588 that Christopher Marlowe (a notorious spy and propagandist for Elizabeth) wrote and oversaw the performance of his play 'The Tragicall History of the Life and Death of Doctor Faustus', in which a learned scholar is tempted into witchcraft, conjures demons and Lucifer himself, and ultimately brings about his own damnation. Marlowe's play made witches entirely real for both his educated and uneducated Protestant audiences, made witches truly terrifying and, most importantly, provided implicit justification for the persecution of the 'witches' hiding amongst us. As under

Henry, men were as capable as women of Catholicism and or witchcraft; hence, both men and women were imprisoned and executed for idolatrous witchcraft by Elizabeth.

The Protestant Elizabeth also had to contend with the threat to her English throne from her Catholic elder cousin Mary, who was the Queen of Scotland 1542-67. After years of plots, schemes and politicking, Mary was eventually forced to abdicate in 1567 in favour of her Protestant son James. It was in the same year that Elizabeth took Mary into 'protective custody'. Yet Mary still had numerous supporters and continued to be implicated in plots against Elizabeth, until Mary was finally executed in 1587. Unsurprisingly, the execution caused outrage amongst Catholics and Mary's supporters in the north of England and in Scotland, and the resulting ongoing dissent in turn contributed towards/ prompted the Protestant James VI of Scotland personally overseeing the witch trials or around one hundred male and female witches in North Berwick. Six 'witches' were executed, but not until the confessions 'extracted' from them had named James VI's cousin Francis Stuart, 5th Earl of Bothwell, as being head of a witches' coven in James's court that plotted to kill the King and seize the throne. It was precisely at this time that Francis Stuart had begun to ally himself with Catholic lords in Scotland. Francis Stuart ultimately fled into exile, but James was now certain he needed to continue to weed out and purge witches from both his court and the wider country. Whether James was driven by an irrational paranoia, a religious belief in witches or an acute political understanding of how just the idea of witchcraft could be used as a pretext for persecuting any threats to his power... hardly matters... and perhaps the three driving reasons all fed into each other to such an extent that they were one and the same thing to him. In 1596, James wrote and published *Daemonologie*, a treatise which asserted the genuine existence of witches and described witchcraft as 'high treason against God'. No effort was to be spared in the uncovering of witches and no mercy was to be shown. The reign of terror was about to begin. The Great Scottish Witch Hunt of 1597 saw trials taking place all across Scotland. At least 400 people were put on trial for witchcraft and or diabolism. It is believed approximately two hundred 'witches' were executed in that year alone.

When Elizabeth died in 1603, King James VI of Scotland inherited the English throne, becoming King James I of England and Scotland. The increase in his power and kingdom only saw the number of threats (imagined or otherwise) to him increase. James's persecution of witches was to continue unabated. His Witchcraft Act of 1604 was entitled *An Act against Conjuration, Witchcraft and dealing with evil and wicked spirits*, and insisted upon the death penalty for anyone who simply invoked spirits or communed with familiar spirits. The definition of witchcraft was now so broad that it gave James licence to have absolutely anyone who met with his disapproval branded a witch and thence executed. In 1606, Shakespeare's 'Macbeth' was only to add propagandist fervour and fuel to the fire. The hunting and persecution of witches was soon to reach its very height. In 1612, ten 'witches' (eight women and two men) in Pendle, Lancashire, were found guilty by a court and executed. The act of 1604 was then to be enforced by one Matthew Hopkins, the English self-styled Witchfinder General. Hopkins and his associates were particularly active in East Anglia and are believed to have been responsible in just two years (1646-48, years during which Puritan intolerance held sway in England) for more people (300) being hanged/ executed for witchcraft in England than had occurred in that country in the previous hundred years. In addition, further witch hunts were to take place in Scotland, in 1628-31, 1649-50 and 1661-62. In total, estimates put the number of witches burned in Scotland between the years 1450 and 1750 at approximately 4000 people, an incredible number considering that Scotland's entire population in 1600 only stood at 800,000.

Although King James I of England and Scotland died in 1625, what he put into motion saw thousands of innocent people and witches persecuted and killed. The grief, anguish and fear that was visited upon the surviving families, friends, loved ones and communities of the victims must have taken in all but the entire country. Neither should we forget the 19 people who were executed across the Atlantic as a result of the Puritan witch trials in Salem, New England, 1692-93. The last execution of witches that took place in England were of three women in Bideford, Devon, in 1683. The women were convicted based on hearsay, of course. A plaque dedicated to 'the hope of an end to persecution and tolerance' commemorates them at Exeter's Rougemont Castle, where the witch trials were held. Laws against witchcraft were repealed in an Act of Parliament in 1735, although it did still impose fines and possible imprisonment upon those who might claim magical powers. That act was repealed in 1951 by the Fraudulent Mediums Act, which was in turn repealed in 2008.

The Witches of Boscastle

It is worthy of note that the last execution of witches in England took place in the south-west. The south-west had its own pre-Christian folk tales of pixies/piskies, imps and fairy folk, and its own historical tradition of actual witches and 'kenning or cunning folk'. The witches of the south-west were not simply a creation or fabrication arising from false or political accusation.

No, they were celebrated, respected and valuable members of a significant number of Cornish communities. It is a matter of historical record that such witches existed, their names, dwelling places and spiritual practice fully documented and corroborated.

Crucially, the witches of Cornwall were not considered malign agents of Satan. In this remote region of the country, a region that has never been successfully conquered by the various invaders who had overtaken and 'civilized' the rest of England, both Christianity and modern medicine were slow to arrive. As a result, Cornwall's ancient culture, oral traditions and spiritual beliefs survived far better than the equivalent in other parts of England.

The term 'witch' is used in Cornwall, to be sure, but the terms 'kenning or cunning folk' and 'fey or fairy folk' are used just as often. 'Kenning or cunning folk' were those who had an uncommon understanding, knowledge or sense of nature such that they could cast spells to cure ailments, locate lost objects and livestock, manipulate the elements and ward away evil or bad luck. 'Fey or fairy folk' were capable of much the same, but they were also sensitive to the realm 'beyond', to the extent that they could commune with the spirits and few that resided there, and could sometimes even see or visit that realm, a realm usually forbidden to mortals while they still lived. Hence, the witch of Arthurian legend, Morgana, is nearly always referred to as Morgana le Fey. It is interesting that, although we know of named male witches from Cornwall, the spiritual tradition of Cornish witchcraft is largely a matriarchal one, for the witches frequently invoked the aid of Mother Nature, 'The Goddess' (whose symbol was the moon, that body which governs the female biological cycle) or Queen Mab, she who ruled over the piskies and other fey.

Much Arthurian legend is of course rooted in Cornwall. The castle of Tintagel is purported to have been a seat of the Welsh Uther Pendragon and where Arthur was conceived. Predictably enough, Merlin's Cave is to be found beneath the castle. According to Arthurian legend, St Michael's Mount was the main seat of power of the lost kingdom of Lyonesse, which extended all the way to the Isles of Scilly, until some catastrophic event saw a tidal wave drown most of the land and leave the Mount as a towering island just off the coast. The island can be reached by a 'secret' causeway that is revealed at low tide. Some believe that the lost kingdom to be an equivalent of the fairy realm and that the Mount is the Isle of Avalon, access to which is permitted only to 'fey or fairy folk' and those who are 'kenning or cunning' or in possession of special knowledge, and only as they are permitted by the Lady of the Lake (of Arthurian legend), The Goddess, Mother Nature and Queen Mab.

A mere five miles along the coast from Tintagel is the ancient harbour of Boscastle. Its village is organised along the darkly dramatic gorge of a river that cascades and winds down to the sea, a weaving water course which also provides the only naturally protected deep-water harbour along Cornwall's northern coast. Craggy and forbidding though the place is, it also provides shelter. As boats negotiate the tumultuous and foaming seas waves in order to enter the mouth of the inlet, they are anointed by the Witch's Spout, a powerful jet of water that issues from a blow hole in the rock as the swell surges and rises. Thus blessed, the boats are taken around the first turn of the cliff-walled river and into the preternatural calm and still shelter of Boscastle. There have been sea witches in Boscastle as long as there have been people. Visiting boatmen would buy bespelled pieces of knotted rope so that, upon leaving, they could untie the knots and be gifted the wind to fill their sails and take them safely beyond the sharp and tearing rocks. The Museum of Witchcraft and Magic is based in the centre of the village and operates as both a cultural and educational centre.

The New Witch

With the increasing secularisation and multiculturalism of society, there has been a correlating increase in the tolerance for alternative religions and witchcraft. Where once the Brothers Grimm (1812-57) were morally editing and deliberately Christianising the German, pagan-tradition folk tales they were collecting, 'other'-ing and demonising powerful female characters such as the step-mother, step-sisters, the wise woman of the woods and the maiden-aunt in fairy tales like *Snow White* and *Sleeping Beauty*, now we have more positive witches in the form of Samantha in the *Bewitched* TV show (1964-72), the *Sabrina: The Teenage Witch* comic book and TV shows (1969-present), Terry Pratchett's *Wyrd Sisters* (1988), Hermione in the *Harry Potter* franchise (1997 onwards) and the *Charmed* TV shows (1998-present). Where Disney's early *Snow White* (1937) and *Sleeping Beauty* (1959) animations were popular for their use of the 'wicked witch' trope from the Grimm fairy tales of the same name, now Disney has proactively rewritten and rehabilitated the 'witch' character from *Sleeping Beauty* in the movies *Maleficent* (2014) and *Maleficent: Mistress of Evil* (2019).

One may wonder if the above tendency suggests a move towards a more post-Christian era in the West, as discussed in the book *The Satanic in Science Fiction and Fantasy*. *The Guardian* newspaper (UK) reported in November 2018 that only 722,000 people attend the Church of England's Sunday services, surely an all-time low for the last five hundred years. Over half the UK population reported that they no longer belong to any religion. At the same time, there is now more open practice and public celebration of new age religions, including Wicca/Pagan Witchcraft, than ever before. As early as the 1990s, the UK city of Milton Keynes provided government land to a Wiccan coven so that they had a place where they could freely pursue their ritual and spiritual practice. And the numbers attending Stonehenge for the summer solstice increase year on year.

For many, the above represents social progress, new social freedoms and the recognition of fundamental human rights. Certainly, the feminist cause has thereby made advances, as well as intersectional LGBTQ groups, since the reality of being a demonised, marginalised, exoticized or 'other'-ed individual in society can be identified with by each of us in some respect. And each of us shares in that pre-Christian aspect of our shared cultural identity and cultural heritage that still recognises and thrills at the celebrations marking the change of the seasons and natural world on the pagan calendar: from the Winter Solstice (Yule), to Imbolc (the start of spring/Candlemas), the Spring Equinox (Ostara/Easter), Beltane (the start of summer/May Day), the Summer Solstice (Mid-summer), Lammas (the start of the August harvest season), Mabon (the August Equinox/ Harvest Festival) and Samhain (Hallowe'en).

It is precisely in such a spirit of celebration that we present this collection that is *The Book of Witches*. The stories included explore particular eras of history and society, the suffering and strength of those persecuted for who they are, the wonder of those who discover self-empowerment, and the magic of experiencing this thing we call life. We hope you find the tales herein inspiring, exhilarating, spine-tingling, refreshing and, occasionally, delightfully dark.

Dr Adam Dalton-West, November 2019,
Golder's Green, London, UK

The House in Brooklyn

By Nadine Dalton-West

The neighbourhood of Bushwick has always been a live-and-let-live kind of place. Old men who only speak Yiddish rub shoulders with yoga moms, and boys who brew craft beer that doesn't taste of beer, and tastes instead of acid and herbs, mingle on sidewalks with other boys who actually sell acid and herb, and who keep their hands in their pockets and their eyes on the horizon. The brownstones are snug and the whole place smells of burnt perfumes that come from the soap factory and hang round in a blackened-lavender cloud, and then there is the toasted-acrid scent of pigeon lofts, and the endless applause of pigeon wings, and then there is The House on Upper Cornelia Street.

The House on Upper Cornelia Street has a steep roof with a tilting chimney stack. It has cheery, gabled windows, neat curtains, and a wooden porch that looks surprising in a lane of so many nine-stepped stoops in neat rows, so that if you stand at the intersection and look up the hill, you can see them disappearing into an infinity of geometric illustration. Those would be the first things you noticed, as you looked up.

As you looked down, you would probably notice the chicken legs.

(You might not notice the women: one young, in the upper window, with white blonde hair; one old, silvered, leaning on the sill of the downstairs window. There is a kitchen behind her. Inside it, drifting lazily towards the kerb, is the scent of good soup.)

Nobody remembers when The House on Upper Cornelia Street – or, shall we be friendly? The House – first arrived. The rise and fall of two bright yellow chicken legs was probably unusual even then. If it had been in the 1880s, the ladies in headscarves from the shtetls would have looked sideways at the glistening, scaly legs, and muttered a small curse, and known what was what. In the 1920s, The House would have perturbed the young gang runners in waistcoats, shirtsleeves and caps, and made them clutch for the handles of the knives they thought were a secret. In the 1960s, The House might have become a pilgrimage during the summer of love, and bare-chested hippies might have flocked there to show off their commitment to peace and acceptance, or anyway, the kind of peace and acceptance you can offer to a gargantuan pair of chicken legs which flex and bend and twitch their chicken knees, as long as they make sure to stand still, goddamnit, and not to come anywhere too close.

As it is, The House has at least twelve Instagram pages. There it is, overfiltered in Amaro, as #chickenhouseUSA; there, dressed in slightly more sepia, as #BestofBrooklynHouse; here, in high-contrast black and white from all angles apart from straight on, as #TheArtHouse19. Gaggles of girls pose outside it, shrill with half-feigned terror, taking selfies: wide-angled, always; they want to get as much of The House in as possible, to show they were brave, that they were truly there. They never notice, as they contort their shoulders and chins to achieve their practised angles, that the house wiggles and tilts in its turn. It has its own angles. It likes the way the sunlight brings out its lintels.

When The House flexes, or sits suddenly in a puff of city dust, the Instagram girls scatter like birds after a gunshot.

***

"Vassilia?"

"Yes, Baba?"

"The cat has brought another poor kill to me. This will not do."

"Nay, Baba. I will talk to him." Vassilia opens her eyes, stretches her arms and legs, and stands. She looks towards the door, which is making a low, grinding sound with its teeth. "Puss?" she says, and "Koshka?" again, as she looks into the corners of the living room. When she spies the black cat, he winks at her with his one good amber eye, and then yawns. His tongue and mouth gape pinkly, and his fangs twinkle. Vasa gazes at the floor in front of him, where a small, hairless thing lies bleeding. She nudges it with her foot.

From behind her, a curtain rattles on its tracks, and a heavy clip, clip, clip sound of footsteps approaches.

"Look it here. Is it a diseased rat? Here, in my home? Manged and palsied, look at it, and why does my cat bring me this insult?"

Vasa smiles. "Nay, Baba. It is a fashionable dog again." She looks calmly at Baba, whose face in some lights looks twisted and gnarled, with a terrifying nose that droops over her pointed chin, and sharp, tiny teeth that snap and snarl, and which in other lights looks nothing more than the face of any old woman, any at all. "See? Not sick. Just naked."

"He look sick to me," mutters Baba. The cat arches itself, lengthens, lies down beside its kill and licks its paws. It seems unconcerned. "Why," Baba continues, as she bends and grasps the dead thing by its wrinkled scruff, "do these Americans make pets of these sickly things? Animal cannot defend, no good for human food, what is its purpose?"

"Wearing a jumper on the internet, I think," says Vasa. She allows herself a moment to imagine their Koshka slinking into a refurbished apartment through a window, and eyeing up the tiny handbag hound with its one glimmering eye. The idea pleases her. She follows Baba into the kitchen. Beneath their feet, a little earthquake: the house has been standing on one leg for a time, for reasons best known to itself. The sudden thumping adjustment indicates it has returned to a two-footed position. Baba and Vasa roll like sailors in high seas. They are used to it. Baba slams the carcase down onto her workbench, and picks up a knife; with one, practised move, she slits the throat in a perfect circle and skins the thing like a rabbit. The knife flickers, one, two, three strokes. One good pull and off comes the skin like wax off a ripe cheese.

"Hang that," she says, and Vasa does. It is soft, and will be good for gloves. Now Baba uses her cleaver: bang, bang, snick, bang. She fillets the thing for cat food, makes neat parcels for the larder from beeswax paper, and at the last, throws the head into the trash. It sits there for a moment, a startled expression in its gaping, bulbous eyes, before sliding down the pile of potato peelings, slowly out of view.

It is only when they have finished butchering the dog that they become aware that the house is clicking its teeth. The door to The House looks, in some lights, like a cavernous mouth with iron bolts for teeth, sharpened into points that could pierce unwary flesh, and in other lights looks like nothing more than a brightly painted wooden door, like any door at all. "What ails you?" asks Baba? Clickety-schnick, go the teeth, and so she washes the dog blood from her hands at the sink and then goes to the window.

Staring back at her, one hand shading his eyes from the

watery sunlight, is a man in a grey suit and highly polished black shoes. In the other hand, he clutches a briefcase.

Baba flings open a window. This seems to startle the man, who flinches at the sound and flaps the briefcase up and down in front of him. "Hello?" he says. His voice rises into a whine on the final vowel.

"You sound like an ailing sheep," says Baba.

"I do?" asks the man. "I mean, is it alright if I have a word with the owner? Is that you, ma'am? Our paperwork is…," and he flaps the case up and down again, "a little unclear."

"Is it? Is it?" Baba nods deeply, and strokes her chin. Vasa suppresses a snort. Then Baba slaps the door-jamb and says, "Down," and Vasa holds on to the kitchen table. The House sighs, shifts, and then lowers itself, meeting the floor with a bump. Outside, the grey man flinches again, but holds his ground. When the house has settled, he takes six slow steps forwards until he is inside the yard.

"I'm Martin Merson, ma'am. I work at City Hall? Are you the property owner?"

"Of this house?"

"Yes ma'am."

Baba leans forwards. "This house has no owner, Martin Merson. Who could own such a house?"

"Well, by law, someone has to…own…property," he says.

"Do they? Do they?" asks Baba, nodding sagely. "That is very interesting, Mr Merson. But if your papercase cannot tell us who owns this…property, as you say, then how can we help you?"

He chews the inside of his cheeks for a moment. "There is something of a planning permission issue, ma'am. We can't find any record of you having permission to erect…" With his free hand, he gestures up and down. Beneath Vasa, there is a barely perceptible juddering, the kind that might come, hypothetically, from a house giggling silently to itself.

She rises, and joins Baba at the window. "Mr Merson," she says. "We can't summon an owner from the ether, I'm afraid. We don't have one locked in a cellar. What would you like us to do?"

Merson's brow has begun to glisten under the April sun. He dabs at his hairline with his pale palm. "Well. Miss. Without a record of planning permission, I'm afraid the city has no choice but to…"

"I see."

Merson kneels in the yard dust. He unclips his briefcase, opens the lid and extracts a thin envelope. He lifts it in the air with both hands. Vasa can feel Baba smiling. She is used to this kind of supplication. "This is the letter," he says.

"Leave it there," says Vasa.

"I'm supposed to hand it to the owner."

"Ah, life," says Baba. "So full of painful compromise."

Merson places the letter on the ground. He scrabbles to his feet, backs out of the yard, and marches away as fast as his shiny shoes can carry him.

Baba and Vasa keep a tight grip on the windowsill. Beneath them, the floor rolls and flexes, as the house shreds the envelope with its sharp claws.

∗∗∗

It is said that in 1662 a huntsman found the home of Baba Yaga in a birch forest, where he had become lost on a hunt for a great silver stag. Upon his return to the city, he told his tale to the landlord, who told it to the white-blonde maid, who told it to the duke she was sleeping with, who owned that birch forest and everything within it. "I cannot abide this," the duke cried, "for every man knows that the woman of the forests is dangerous, and her home an abomination, and that she must be driven out." He pulled at his sheets, causing the white-blonde maid to fall from his bed with a yelp and a thump. And he saddled his horse, took up his sword, and commanded his boy to do likewise. Together they rode into the forest, the duke clad in splendour, the boy with his voice at the turn between boy and man, following the path as the maid had described.

Once inside the forest, however, they lost their way. They became separated, and although the boy called out, the duke could not find him. So they both went on, each horse stepping slowly and carefully through the shadows.

Deep, deep inside the forest, the boy saw, strung out along the narrow pathway, lanterns that glimmered brightly. He saw that each lantern was a skull, and that a flame without a fuel burned from behind the eyes, and that each skull shone beams of light like fireflies, or stars, or beacons. And he was an honest boy, and faithful, and so he bowed to each lantern he passed, and wished peace upon the spirits who had once inhabited each skull, and thanked them for their service. It is said, too, that the duke passed much the same way, and saw the path illuminated before him. And it is said that the duke spat upon the ground, and said, "Faugh, this bitch turns my land into a charnel house," and that he kicked out from his saddle and struck each skull with his foot, as he passed.

As time went on, it is said, the duke was stopped upon the path by a cat, very vilely made and bony to look upon, with one large, glowing eye. And that cat mewed for food, or aid. The duke, so it is said, was repulsed by the verminous thing, and rode his horse hard toward it, until the iron horseshoes clipped the animal's mangy tail and it fled, yowling, into the night. The boy, who passed much the same way, also pulled up his horse when he saw the cat, and he saw – because he was a good boy, and faithful – that the cat was small and harmless, and that it gazed with no malice from that one good eye. And the boy dismounted and rubbed the cat in that place which pleases them, above the nose and between the eyes, and he fed the cat a piece of bacon from his ration, and the cat rubbed its head on his shins and purred mightily, and then trotted away.

Eventually, after many winding turns of the path, both reached a clearing. In the clearing, a hut. On the steps of the hut, an old woman with silver hair that swept the ground. When she saw the duke, she asked, "Do you come to Baba for ill, or for good?"

"I come to rid my lands of you," he said. "You bring harm to my people and corruption to my lands. And you do not have my permission to remain, by my decree."

"Do I?" said the woman. It is said that she smiled, and that a small, black cat climbed onto her lap and washed itself. "But was it not you who brought harm into the forest? Not you who shattered my lanterns and left the pathways dark and dangerous? Not you who attacked a defenceless animal?"

It is said that the duke pulled himself up in his saddle. "I did nothing of the sort," he declared.

"And as for permission," said the woman, "think carefully before you answer. Does everything in this forest require your permission to exist within it?"

"Of course! It is my forest. My land!"

"Well then," said the woman. "You had better get to work."

It is said that she did not move a silver hair on her head. But that before her eyes, the duke transformed into a fat and dowdy grouse, perched on top of his horse like an onion on a biscuit.

"You will fly with difficulty, dull bird. You will trudge along the ground throughout your forest until you have given permission to every tree, every bird, every scurrying thing, to be here in your land." And the woman rose and flicked the bird to the floor. It scuttled into the undergrowth.

It is said that the duke's horse made many weeks' worth of fine stews, and that the grouse may still be there, granting his permissions tree by tree, even to this day.

Now, when the boy arrived in the clearing, he found a hut and, on the steps of that hut, a woman with silver hair that swept the ground. He dismounted from his horse and said, "Isvinye, madam. I have lost my master in this wood, where he instructed me to follow him."

"Do you come to Baba for ill or for good?" the old woman asked him.

"I come because I was told to," the boy said, because he was an honest boy, and faithful. "But I hope I have no ill intentions."

At this, she smiled, and a black cat jumped from her lap and swayed towards the boy, mewing in recognition. "You have brought good to this place," Baba said. "You have been respectful of its dead things, and generous to its living things." She did not move a hair on her head, but when he turned to look at his horse, he saw that his old nag had become a handsome thoroughbred, saddled with rich leather and bearing saddlebags which looked heavy, and full. Baba nodded. "You will find your way back to your village, because I have said it will be so. There is an empty manor house there, I believe, for one who arrives quickly and with coin to hire good staff."

So he did. When he arrived, he found that there was already a young woman there, with white blonde hair and silver eyes, and she kept house, and kept other things too: secrets, and his young heart.

But that is another tale, child, for another day.

Back on Upper Cornelia street, the House has gone to sleep. It can be inconvenient to live in a house which can sometimes draw down its own blinds and then embark upon an afternoon's robust snoring, but there you have it. Baba and Vasa make do, and speak up.

"What does he want, eh?" Baba asks. She holds an electric lighter up to the tobacco in a clay pipe. It hisses and fizzes its way to combustion.

"Planning permission," says Vasa.

"Not a word I am fond of."

"I recall," says Vasa. She leans back in her chair.

Baba blows out a long white stream of smoke, which coils in the air. It smells of cherrywood. "So what do we do?"

"We could move. We could stay. Have you thought about going back to the woods for a time? It might be a quieter life." Vasa gazes thoughtfully at the cat. "Fewer irate neighbours wondering where their chihuahuas are, anyway."

"Too quiet. Too many birds."

"You like birds."

"They talk incessantly. And they have little to contribute. Besides, how would I help my people, in the woods?" Baba stands, pipe in hand, and walks across the small living space, pulling back the curtain which separates the kitchen. "Come," she says. "Work to do."

And Vasa rises, and work they do. In other times and places, in the woods, the young men and women who come to Baba do so sporadically, after tedious hours of riddles and anthropomorphised wildlife beneath the canopy of trees. Here, in Brooklyn, they form an orderly queue. "It is nice," says Baba, "to have a bat land on your shoulder and ask you why the sun rises in the East. But it is far from necessary." And she speaks the truth. Baba can tell you why you are sick, or why you cannot conceive a child, or what to do about the one you have conceived in error, without much ritual at all. At the front of the house, the pouting girls take their selfies. At the back of the house, Baba throws open the stable door for business.

The line is strange, because half of the people in it do not want anyone to know that they are in it. There is a lot of conspicuous shuffling, facing in unusual directions, and overt examination of sidewalks and street art. The people maintain irregular distances, and sometimes the queue is more like a work of modern art as it snakes down Cornelia Street and back onto Wilson. But every man and woman in it knows who is next, and when they need to shuffle forwards. Word of Baba's help is a great leveller: slick Montcler hoods approach the stable door, and so do faded Walmart hoodies. Baba speaks with them all. More than that: she sees. When a young man with cracked and bleeding hands is before her, she offers him a poultice made from fine herbs and beeswax. He will heal. When a young man with cracked and bleeding lips stands there, she listens to what he eats and who he copulated with, and tells him about vitamins and prophylactics. He will heal too.

When a young man with a cracked and bleeding heart stands there, she sees him. Those cases are harder. Does he come to Baba for good or for ill? Vasa watches these ones intently. She knows that she can make the blended herbs for the poultices or ointments, and that she can strain and pound at stone and bark to extract the minerals needed for healing. She even knows, after an apprenticeship longer than can be spoken, how to see signs of hidden sickness in the body. (Skin, hair, mouth, guts, teeth, eyes: the human body is much like that of a large dog, when all is said and done, and it tells its tales in the same language.) But the ailing soul – ah, that is where the best mysteries lie. That is an endless book in a foreign tongue, with pages made of mercury and falsehood, and Vasa has yet to learn to read it with more than a child's fluency. Instead, she watches and listens, and is silent. Baba asks him questions, and listens not to the answers, but around them. Baba can hear the colours of misery, melancholy, hubris, and ennui. Her prescriptions seem simple, and are the opposite of that.

Forgive yourself. Then, really, actually forgive yourself.

Believe that they tried their best, inside the limits of their ability.

The delusion that you could have changed events through your actions is suffocating you.

Do not try to trap happiness. Happiness is a vagabond. It will stumble across you, from time to time.

Everyone has ill intentions: create some house rules for yours.

If you ask for more than people can give, you will believe that everyone owes you something.

Let yourself be alone and silent with yourself. It will terrify you.

Vasa used to think that they were useless homilies. Inspirational greetings-card slogans for the credulous to buy and pin to the cork board that they use instead of a conscience. She has learned from close observation that they are not. The right words spoken quietly to the right soul can drain a person's face of blood, and see them shake their heads and distort their brows, and as they writhe and cringe Baba takes them by the hands and murmurs something to them. That part, Vasa cannot hear. Often, they weep.

But when they leave, the soul-sore, the sunlight shines on their tear-streaked faces and there is illumination there, where previously there had been only dullness.

The sunlight is low now: the sky has become milky, the trees bend in the wind, and the warmth bleaches out of the air. Baba starts to dust down her counter and pack away the small cloth parcels into her wooden chest. Vasa unties the scarf from around her head and lets her hair fall down, massaging her scalp to take away the soreness.

It is then, through the stillness, that she sees the grey cars. There are two, making their way up Cornelia Street, nosing remorselessly along the white median line like dogs on the hunt. When they reach the lamp-post before the House, they swing lazily towards the kerbside and stop. A small cluster of Instagram girls taking sunset photographs scatter, as if sensing danger. The first car's door pops open with a dull, flopping sound, and the man in the grey suit steps out. Martin Merson, holding not his briefcase now, but a long black tube on a strap, the kind that holds architects' plans, or City Hall zoning maps. From the second car, another man emerges; he is equally grey, but taller, lanker, like an ill tree. The two men lean towards each other and talk. The lank man covers his mouth. Merson nods. His hand jerks convulsively in the direction of the House, and then both men turn to stare directly at the place where Vasa stands. The tube of documents is cocked towards her, like a gun. Then the lank man takes his cell phone and begins to take photographs with it. He walks up and down the sidewalk, his flash popping ineffectually in the twilight.

Vasa blinks a little, in this miniature lightning storm.

Martin Merson stares, all the while.

The House growls. The House knows a predator when it sees one. Baba appears at Vasa's shoulder, and rests her wiry hand on the windowsill. The three of them watch together as the lank man approaches the fence, holding something plastic and something metal, one in each hand. They both glisten unhealthily. Then the man moves his wrists and fingers and there are four sharp bangs, and Vasa can see now that he has stapled a laminated notice to the wooden fence-post next to the gate.

The grey men step back to observe their work, and then

retreat to the cars, which grumble into life and then crawl slowly back down Cornelia Street, leaving only a fug of diesel hanging in the air.

"Should we read it?" ask Vasa.

"We don't need to read it," says Baba. "I know lord of manor beginning the hunt when I see one."

"Then what shall we…"

Baba raises a finger. They watch, in silence, as two of the young Instagram girls approach the fence and bend over to read the notice, warily, as though they are afraid of being caught. One of them pulls out a phone, and the rectangle glows briefly in the half-light. "I think," Baba says, "that I perhaps have idea."

***

The hashtag #savethehouse begins trending at 9:04 the following morning.

By 10:30, there is a small group gathered outside. They are mostly made up of Brooklyn's more eccentric citizens, and there is definite evidence of one unicycle, two cava-poos in chest-carriers, and an unspecified quantity of free-floating marijuana. But by midday, the numbers are growing. The first placard arrives at 12:15 and reads, "Hands off our House." It has a drawing of a unicorn on it. Baba and Vasa raise an eyebrow at the non-sequitur, but agree to let it pass. Shortly thereafter, a young man appears with his own supplies of boards-on-sticks and a roll of marker pens, which he unfurls on the sidewalk.

Half an hour passes, in which the growing crowd of protesters assumes an unusual position: somewhere north of a hundred people kneel over sheets of paper, and the sidewalk looks like a kindergarten art lesson. Somebody, somewhere, hums a happy tune.

When they begin to stand again, they lift their newly-created placards. Vasa and Baba spend a merry half hour reading aloud. "Equal rights in Brooklyn Heights," reads one, geographically confused sign. "A bird in the hand is worth two in Bushwick," declares another. ("Is both clever and meaningless, at the same time," Baba murmurs, appreciatively.) They both enjoy "Make Chicken Houses Great Again," and cannot quite agree whether the "This is a Witch Hunt" sign is in the best of taste. The cameras begin to click in earnest., as the crowd begins to take selfies of their own faces beneath their own signs. Occasionally, a corner of the House creeps into view in the photographs which are now pinging onto the hashtag thread in their hundreds.

At 1:30, a camera crew arrives from a news channel. Three young women dance around an aging man with hair that sits higher above his scalp than god intended, and flick at his face with powder brushes.

By 2pm, a small scuffle has broken out between a libertarian wing of the protest, who are here to defend the right of any private citizen to bear chicken legs upon American land they have claimed as theirs, and a more liberal wing who believe that planning permission and civic building legislation are inherently discriminatory against minority citizens, including those with chicken legs. Voices are raised, collars grabbed. An arm is flung out in the general direction of Hudson Bay. "Huddled MASSES," yells one voice.

"Yearning to be FREE," counters another. "And anyway, it's not huddled. It's standing up."

Vasa feels a slight tipping of the floorboards, as might be experienced when a house glances down at its own feet.

At 3:45pm, a counter-protest begins. Five middle-aged ladies clutch a bedraggled assortment of infants in front of them, and try to hold aloft a bed-sheet with "Think of the

Children" scrawled across it. This proves harder than it looks, as the various children tug on different corners of the sheet and try to play hide-and-go-seek behind it, and one of them shouts "Mama, look! Chickchick!" in increasingly excited tones. The House skitters its heels around, in a kind of tap-dance, and the child beams.

By 5pm, there is a helicopter overhead. More TV crews have turned up. A young woman has begun a chant about police brutality, more in hope than in anger. She ties herself to the House's fence with a scarf for half an hour and then, when nothing unpleasant has happened, unties herself again.

People have begun to order takeout. Baba and Vasa smile, and begin to heat and season a good rabbit stew. The aroma drifts beyond the windows, past the fence, and into the street.

All along the sidewalks, in the early evening sun, the part rage-part picnic protest sits down to eat.

**

Martin Merson appears as night is falling. He picks his way through the happy clusters of protesters and skirts around the news crews. Someone has brought speakers along, and a warm arpeggio of acoustic guitar weaves around the assembled crowds, the way a curious and friendly cat might. Someone else has bought up the tiki torches from the hardware store two blocks away, and they flicker gently, orange and red. The night is soft and humid.

Baba stands at the window and touches her fingertips together. "Dobr'veycher," she greets him.

"Ma'am," he replies. "This is an illegal protest. It is against regulations."

"To be sure," she answers. "I cannot tell you every line of your laws. If it is written that these people cannot eat supper on these pavements, then so it must be."

"It is not…" He flares his nostrils. "There are no permits for this. You are *responsible* for this."

"Am I?" Baba taps her fingertips together, a ripple from one end of her steepled fingers to the thumbs. "But I made only my own supper."

Merson takes one step from the sidewalk. He puts one foot and then the other inside the yard. A quiet whisper begins from the crowd, just the slightest susurrus, as he crosses the line in the dust. "This is a sit-in," he yelps. "In support of…this." He waves his hand, so pale it is nearly blue, and naked-looking without its briefcase or its staple-gun, towards the House. "They have no permission for this protest."

From where Vasa is standing, with the House tensed and drawn up to its full height, he looks like a creature from Animal Planet, seen from a helicopter far above. Like a grey bird, quorking. His mouth opens and closes. Baba's voice is like a purr. "So you don't want them to sit?"

The whisper from the crowd builds. There is a sense of approaching rain. One by one, they begin to stand.

Merson looks around, turns, and takes another step, backwards this time, into the yard. "Wait," he says. "I didn't say…"

As they stand, the people who have bought tiki torches lift them. If you squint, they look almost like small skulls, glowing through all of the dark spaces with a fantastical light.

"So," says Baba. "They don't sit."

The music stops, suddenly. The gentleness is turning into something different, and Merson is still moving towards the house, deeper and deeper into the yard, and the crowd begins to low softly, an animal noise of distress, and they move forwards. He lifts his hands in front of him as he backs, step by step, until Vasa loses sight of him beneath the porch, until just his hands remain in view. "They don't have…they need… they're unauthorised," comes the whining voice, higher in pitch now. "You're unauthorised. This whole goddamn…Don't walk towards me. Don't threaten me. Make them sit back down."

"How can I make them do such a forbidden thing?" asks Baba. She leans forwards, bending to see the man in the shadows.

"Make them stop!"

"No, Mr Martin Merson. They are not my people. Everyone here belongs to themselves. You must tell them what you want." And then Baba straightens up and grips the window-frame, very tightly, until her knuckles whiten, and Vasa blinks, and does the same.

The pale hands of Martin Merson shake. The crowd are slowly moving towards him. Some are almost at the gate. His voice rises in a wild bleat. "Stop and sit down! Everybody here! I order you to *sit down*!"

There is a second's silence. The crowd holds its breath.

The House plummets like a falling elevator.

For one brilliant second, Vasa and Baba float into the air and are suspended there, and it is like flying.

***

It is a live-and-let-live place, this neighbourhood of Bushwick. When the protest is over, and no one can quite remember why they were suddenly standing on Upper Cornelia Street, holding a placard and a half-finished joint, and gazing towards a small, wooden house with a simple chain-link fence and being waved at by two women, one old, one young – when they shake their heads and wonder at the torches and the dust and the news-vans with their confused anchors shouting into their earpieces – they turn and head towards home. Some of them sing softly as they go. They feel bewildered, and they check their Instagram feeds and wonder what this odd hashtag was, and why they have taken a selfie in front of a boring clapperboard two-storey, but they feel content as they walk. After all, there have been flash-mobs before, and there will be flash-mobs again, and who can object to an evening in the warm twilight, with friends, beneath the subtle city stars?

Ever afterwards, the children of Bushwick will remember the legend – although they will never know quite whose older sister or loose-lipped mother told them – and will wear a very distinctive costume that passes down from one Halloween to the next: yellow tights, red shoes, a white wooden hut as a body, and two dangling hands, pale wadding stuffed into a pair of their mom's tights, hanging in front of them.

***

"They get what they ask for," says Baba. "And they never see it coming."

"I know."

Baba takes wood, and stokes the fire, very gently, stirring the embers with a glowing copper poker. She stares at what she sees there, and blinks. "Maybe is now time to go?"

"Perhaps," nods Vasa. The one-eyed cat stretches itself. She draws the curtains and strokes the white walls. They vibrate just a little, in self-satisfaction, or digestion, and who can say which? "It has been a long time. But I still want to see somewhere new. Maybe colder. Maybe fewer people."

"That sounds like home," says Baba.

And so they leave that place, very quietly. And some say that they went home, and some say that they travelled north from that place and wrestled with bears, and that the House wore a goose-tail feather in a hat made of pure, white snow.

And some say that they hunted the unwary with icicles like spears, and that they spilled blood again, somewhere in the arctic circle where it is always midnight, and where Baba flies all night through the darkness.

But these are other tales, child, for another day.

Greenford

(From *The Central Line*)
By Adam Lively

There's a spot in West London where the Grand Union canal is met, in an elegant curve, by one of the main motorways into the city. For a short stretch Westway, on its huge concrete pillars, casts a deep shadow across the towpath. One golden evening in early summer, a young man called Ivan is passing swiftly through this spot – wheels spinning, sunlight flashing off the water, a muffled thunder of traffic somewhere far above him – when a vivid image passes through his mind: he is ten years old, sitting in a sun-filled classroom, obsessively drawing tangents on graph paper. And in the next moment – as canal and motorway part and the towpath runs beside a row of trees – something small and hard falls and hits Ivan on the bridge of his nose.

He skids to a halt. He looks up for a moment at the cloudless blue sky. What is he looking for? A bird? An aeroplane? Then he looks down at the towpath and sees the culprit: a hazelnut. He rubs his nose and slides his gaze to the still waters of the canal. *What*, he thinks to himself, *are the chances of that?*

***

Gulls wheel and scream across a cloudless sky. Twelve-year-old Ivan is sitting on the shingle with Donna De Freitas, the younger sister of his best friend Paul. Paul is wandering about further down the beach, singing to himself. Up by the road, Paul and Donna's mother and father are sitting on a bench feeding Tommy, the baby. Ivan and Donna are throwing pebbles against a concrete breakwater, watching them accumulate. The falling pebbles sound an endless, brittle click. The sunlight off the sea is dazzling.

***

Ivan's eyes flicker between two large screens. His fingers flutter over the computer keyboard. Spectral thumbnails slide across the screens and down to the timeline, which shifts and expands to accommodate them. When he has made his trims, he sits back and watches a loop of the edit, studying the object he has created. He gets up, stretches, and walks out of the edit suite, along the corridor, and into the machine room. He stands before the banks of blinking, coloured lights. Ten minutes later he is still standing there. He should be getting back to work. But instead, a vague, purposeless thought is turning itself over and over in his mind like a mantra: behind those lights, there are thousands of chunks of frozen time.

***

As summer goes on, Ivan feels an old, dark mood begin to descend. His sleep is bothered by dreams. He wakes at four and watches the dawn through thin curtains. At the end of the day, when he cycles home to his flat along the canal, he finds himself slowing down, lost in thought, until he comes to a halt and dismounts to sit on a bench and stare for an hour or more at the dark, motionless water. He needs to be alone. He turns down invitations from friends. He pursues thoughts that turn into labyrinths. His friends notice the change in him and urge him to take a break. In July a group of them are going to a festival at a place called Greenford, in Cornwall. It's a small festival – off the beaten track and New Age-y. Why doesn't he take a few days off and come too? At first, he resists. He's never liked festivals. He doesn't like crowds. All he wants to do, right now, is sit and think.

But on the evening before the festival is due to begin, when his friends have already left, he changes his mind. Sitting by the canal again, gazing once more at the water, he suddenly sees where the path he is on will lead him: he'll stop going to work, he'll end up sitting by the canal from dawn to dusk with a can of Special Brew on the bench beside him… So he gets back on his bike, cycles home to Acton and buys a ticket for the festival online. Luckily, he's owed a couple of days' holiday and things are quiet at the post-production house. Next morning, he phones in. He stuffs some clothes into a backpack and rides down to the West Country on his motorbike. He speeds down the fast lane of the M4, flashing cars out of the way. When he reaches the gates of the festival, following yellow AA signs down steep-banked country lanes, he feels his whole body seized with tremors. He hasn't eaten for twenty-four hours.

At the entrance to the festival, men in fluorescent tabards talk into headsets, guardedly watching crowds of youths in home-knitted jerseys and dreadlocks. Inside, the atmosphere is low-key. He unwinds. After wandering around for an hour, he comes across one of his friends. He is reunited with the others, welcomed with open arms, given beer and a spliff, and shown where he can crash. He sleeps for ten hours.

Next morning, he sits around for a while, talking with a couple of his friends about the bands who are playing. Then he sets off to explore the site. There are half-a-dozen stages, two avenues of food-stalls, and a bazaar with blandishments for mind, body and spirit. Ivan is standing at the edge of the Tribal Village. Before him there is just one small line of marquees left that he hasn't looked at, stretching up a hill towards the perimeter fence. Beyond the fence the hill continues, fields and hedges, to a dark wood. There is a lull in the music behind him. He stands there, uncertain whether to make the effort of walking up the hill to look at those last marquees.

Two crows launch themselves from a chestnut tree just the other side of the security fence and flap off towards the horizon.

In the time he has spent standing there, he could easily have gone up the row of marquees and back again. But he stands there poised. The moment seems stretched, but without duration: each breath of wind across his face, each shard of sunlight flashing between the trees, is suddenly and simultaneously liberated. Each extends to infinity in its own dimension.

He turns away and makes his way back to the main body of the festival. He feels a strange mixture of reluctance and relief that he can't explain.

That evening his mood changes: his depression has returned. He finds the music oppressively noisy. He seeks out the quietest corners of the site. When people make conversation with him, he moves away. He retires to the tent early and dreams fitfully. He is woken by his friends crashing. He dreams again. He wakes late morning, exhausted.

He returns to the line of marquees at the edge of the site. He starts walking up the slope. The first two marquees are closed up. The next two marquees house clothes stalls – one North African, the other South Asian. But it is early in the day and they are still putting the racks out. Ivan's steps slow.

The last marquee, set apart slightly from the others, appears at first to have no sign on it at all. Then Ivan notices an A4 sheet gaffer-taped to one of the panels.

"CHRONOS"
TIME MAGICK – TEMPORAL HEALING
PLEASE ENTER

He pulls aside the flap and goes in. It seems bigger inside than outside, like the Tardis in *Doctor Who*. The white canvas walls are distant. There is an expanse of white plastic floor. In a far corner a man sits on a folding chair beside a low table. He is dressed all in black. On the table is a large hourglass. The man is knitting some shapeless object, gradually unspooling a large ball of black wool.

Ivan walks towards him. The man sports a goatee, and wears his long black hair, greying slightly, in a ponytail. His face is small, olive-toned and wrinkled. Set in it are two impassive, slate-grey eyes.

Ivan crosses the expanse of white plastic and says, "I was intrigued by your sign". His voice feels like it belongs to someone else.

Chronos puts down his knitting and smiles. The smile is the kind that people make when something they've long suspected has been confirmed.

Ivan looks around. There's nowhere for him to sit. "What's 'temporal healing'?" he asks.

"It means going back," says Chronos. He has a hint of a Midlands accent. "It means putting things right."

"You mean, what do you call it, 'regression therapy'?"

"That's not what I mean," says Chronos. "I mean going back."

Out of the corner of his eye, Ivan notices that the sands in the hourglass are running out. "Actually going back?"

Chronos nods. "Going back."

The words seem to drop down through the earth beneath them. There is a total, intense silence. The festival has withdrawn.

Chronos speaks once more: "I can give you the chance to live your life again."

For weeks Ivan works on a documentary about one of the lesser-known Saudi kings. The programme is intended for a satellite channel based in Riyadh. The dark, guttural sound of Arabic fills the cutting room. Ivan tires of watching archive of men in red check headdresses getting in and out of aeroplanes and attending camel races. Various Saudi executive producers pass through the office – fragrant men in crisp white *thawb*s. They take tea, play with their BlackBerrys and disappear again. No decisions are made. An atmosphere of inertia descends, as though a *harmattan* had silted the edit suite up with sand.

He still has the business card given to him by "Chronos" at the festival. His memory of the incident is confused and partial. He can't remember being given the card, or how he and Chronos had parted. On the last morning of the festival, he had gone back to the row of marquees that led up the hill, but the tent had been gone.

He might have imagined it – on the other hand there was the card. When he'd got back to London, he'd put it on the mantelpiece in his flat, on top of a pile of utility bills. A few weeks later he'd taken it down and put it in his wallet. Every few days, during idle moments, he'd find himself pulling it out and looking at it. It had no phone number or e-mail address – just a street address in Camden Town. He'd looked it up and found that it was near the canal.

***

One morning, on an impulse, he takes a diversion on the way into work and stays on the towpath as far as Camden Town. At a spot where the dark water passes between tall warehouses, spanned by a low iron bridge, he rests his bicycle against the brickwork and sits on a bench. It is high summer – the sky above is an empty electric blue. But the morning sun is still low, and the canal is sunk deep in the shadows of the buildings.

Ivan gazes down at the water. On its surface plays the image of a child's laughing face. There is a road. Lorries ripple across the water. The child turns and runs.

He arrives late for work to find trouble. After weeks of drinking tea and fiddling with their BlackBerrys, the Saudis have roused themselves: drastic changes must be made to the film. Instantly. Usually, in this kind of situation, Ivan thrives on the pressure. Now he feels adrift. When he loops an edit, he finds himself gazing at it, going around and around, for minutes on end. The director puts his head round the door. He is getting worried. Ivan is getting worried. He has a sick, empty feeling at the bottom of his stomach. He doesn't know what is happening. He can't concentrate. His life seems to be simultaneously grinding to a halt and speeding towards a catastrophe.

Every day now he imagines seeing the laughing boy on the surface of the dark canal.

He phones in sick, and fortunately there is another editor available. He cycles back to that stretch of canal near the address on Chronos's card. The Victorian warehouses, converted into open-plan offices, tower over the water. He sits on a bench on the towpath and gazes at the water's motionless surface. His life is sliding down a slope. He gets up and wheels the bicycle away.

***

He still hasn't returned to work. He wheels his bicycle along the street and finds the house. He checks the card. Flat B. He looks up at the house again. The street is one of the few in this part of Camden untouched by gentrification. Small plants sprout from the brickwork. He turns and walks away, wanders the neighbouring streets aimlessly, and finds himself back at the canal.

***

He rings the bell. There is no reply. He stands there for five minutes, then leaves.

***

He rings the bell. There is a long pause, then the sound of footsteps on the stairs. The door opens. It is Chronos. He turns and leads Ivan up the stairs. Ivan is unsure whether Chronos has recognised him from the festival. Chronos hasn't spoken. They enter a small flat on the first floor.

A slab of grey light between the half-open curtains. A sense of disorder. Ivan is led through into a smaller, windowless room at the back of the flat. On the wall is a single short shelf with some books on it. He can't read the titles. Chronos sits down on a chair beside a low table. As he settles himself in the chair, he runs his fingers through his ponytail.

This time there is a chair on the other side of the table. Ivan sits. Between them is the hourglass.

The conversation starts abruptly, as though resuming after a short interruption.

"How does it work?" Ivan asks.

"When the last grain of sand falls into the bottom of the hourglass you go back."

Ivan looks at the hourglass. The sand sits in the bottom chamber.

"I turn the hourglass over," says Chronos, "and when the last grain of sand falls into the bottom of the hourglass you go back."

"When you go back, can you… change things?"

Chronos is gazing at the hourglass. "That's up to you. When you first go back, you'll remember everything about the future. Then you'll start to forget. But you should try not to forget. Forgetting is natural. It's what we do best."

Chronos looks up and flashes an unexpected grin at Ivan. The grin is not so much malicious as alien. There is a long silence.

"Well?" prompts Chronos. He reaches out for the hourglass.

***

It is dusk. He still has not decided. For two days he has been sitting beside the canal. There is a noise inside his head. It has been getting louder. He gets up.

***

"I turn the hourglass over," says Chronos, "and when the last grain of sand falls into the bottom of the hourglass, you go back." He pauses. "Well?"

They are in the flat in Camden. Ivan nods. Chronos leans

across and turns the hourglass over. The sands begin to fall into the lower chamber. They watch. For a long time they sit watching the sands fall into the lower chamber.

Ivan stares at the hourglass. The sands have almost all gone. Their descent has suddenly seemed to accelerate. Then, as the last grain tumbles down, for a moment time seems to slow down. He sees the last grain magnified hugely, tumbling down through the air like a giant, slow rock. He tries to frame a question for Chronos. He tries to speak.

***

From an early age Ivan has been a solitary child. At playgroup he retreats to a corner and occupies himself turning the wheels of a large plastic watermill or drawing swirling patterns with a red crayon. As he grows older, he learns enough sociability to avoid being bullied. But still he prefers to sit alone, listening to music on his iPod, swinging his legs, lost in thought. In his first year at secondary school, his form teacher suggests to his parents that he should be tested for autism. The experts conclude he's not on the spectrum. His parents get divorced. He is an only child.

His only friend at school is Paul De Freitas. Paul's father is originally from Trinidad. He works for the council and plays guitar in a band in his spare time. His mother works part-time as an art teacher. She's originally from Barbados. The De Freitases have practically adopted Ivan as a member of the family. They take him away with them sometimes on weekend breaks. There are three De Freitas children – Paul, Donna and Tommy. Like their dad, they are all into music. Paul is a talented rapper, quick with words, but he also likes to sing in a soulful falsetto, taking the piss out of the lovers' rock his parents listen to. At school he wins prizes for music. Donna is two years younger. She's pretty and Ivan likes to make her laugh. She laughs easily. Or sometimes they just sit together for hours, playing repetitive games. These are the happiest times he can remember from his childhood. And Tommy is the little one.

***

Gulls wheel across a blue sky. They are walking along the sea front. Ivan glances about him nervously. Flashing coloured lights and music blaze from the amusement arcades. The family reaches a road junction and the children stop in a line. Tommy puts out his hand and it is taken by his father. The children wait for a signal, then cross the road together. Ivan watches all this intently.

They go to a fish-and-chip shop. There is a fug of steam, and the warmth of a lot of people crammed into a small space. Ivan is squeezed in next to Tommy, who is on eye-level with him in a highchair. A waitress arrives with their fish and chips. Tommy's mother picks the batter off some fish for him and blows on the fish before handing it to the toddler. Ivan watches them closely.

***

It is the end of a school year, a July day, and everybody is in the school assembly hall. Prize-giving has finished. Ivan's mum has slipped away. Parents and children are milling about. Paul is admiring the trophy he got for music, and Paul's mum and dad are talking to one of the teachers. No longer forced to sit still and listen to grown-ups, Donna and Tommy are chasing each other around. Paul's mum snaps at them a couple of times, then turns to Paul and Ivan and asks them to start taking the little ones home. She'll catch them up, she says, when she's finished talking to the teacher.

Outside, parents and children straggle down the road, away from the school. Donna and Tommy skip on ahead. Ivan and Paul follow slowly behind, talking about which teams are going to be playing on Match of the Day that night. When they have gone a hundred yards or so, Donna drops back and starts talking to Paul about their summer holiday – they are going abroad for the first time. Tommy continues skipping on ahead.

Suddenly, everything around Ivan flares to life. He sees a car turning in at the next intersection. Further down, a traffic warden talks on her mobile. In the small park on the other side of the road a dog runs up and down. There's something claustrophobic here: he feels hemmed in.

Paul and Donna have fallen behind him – they have been joined by a boy from school, and Paul is showing him his music trophy. He turns back: Tommy is skipping on. Ivan quickens his pace to keep up.

He glances round. Now Paul and Donna are about twenty yards behind him. They have almost ground to a halt, examining the trophy with the boy from school. In the time it takes Ivan to look back again, Tommy has skipped further ahead. He is approaching the intersection with the main road. Ivan quickens his pace. Now things are closing in around him much faster. Past and future are being sucked into the Instant. A woman drops her shopping. A tattooed lorry driver's arm hangs out of a cab window. Gears grind.

Ivan runs. Tommy seems to slow as he approaches the main road. *But Ivan knows what is going to happen*. He rushes at Tommy, shouting his name. The boy turns and looks at him, grinning, then sets off again with renewed zest: he thinks Ivan is playing chase. He stumbles forward, laughing, looking back over his shoulder at Ivan, and Ivan rushes forward, arms flailing. (For a split-second he wants more arms. He cannot have enough arms.) He chases Tommy out into the road.

Tommy stops in the middle of the road and turns – triumphant, because Ivan himself has stopped at the edge of the road. For a moment their eyes meet. The little boy's eyes are laughing. Then there is the sound of screaming and squealing brakes. The lorry wipes Tommy out. Like a screen-wipe in the edit suite.

∗∗∗

For months after Tommy's death Ivan hardly speaks. At night the little boy's laughing eyes emerge from the darkness and lock with his own. The sympathy and concern that people offer him only increase his distance from them. He knows what they do not know – or pretend not to know: it was he who killed Tommy.

He cannot bear to be with the De Freitas family. At school, even when the initial shock and anguish and grief have subsided, he cold-shoulders Paul. He turns his back on their friendship.

His academic results are mediocre. Nothing can hold his interest. He spends his spare time watching television. He scrapes enough GCSEs to get into the sixth-form, but his results at A-level are even more disappointing (especially to his parents, who both went to university). He gets a place at the local FE College to do Media Studies.

And then, a few weeks into his course, his life is transformed. He has become friendly with the post-production tutor, and one day the tutor takes him aside and tells him, confidentially, that the course he is on is useless, and that if he wants to make it in the industry the best thing would be to go straight in and learn on the job. The tutor has been watching Ivan and can see that he has aptitude and enthusiasm for editing. He knows a post-production house in Soho that is recruiting runners. He can put Ivan's name forward.

So that is how Ivan's life is changed. He jacks in his course and starts at the post-production house and finds his vocation. He finds friends too, within the small world of editors and technicians. Only occasionally does he stop his bike and stare at the dark, slick surface of the canal.

***

Three years after he has started working at the post-production house, Donna De Freitas gets in touch with him through Facebook. She is doing her teacher training at a college in Holborn. They exchange chatty messages, then arrange to meet one evening at a pub called *The Friend at Hand*, round the back of Russell Square tube station. At first everything is fine. They chat as easily as they had when they were kids. Donna goes to the loo and Ivan buys another round of drinks.

Then Donna starts talking about Paul. She tells him that Paul has just finished a music technology course at the University of Westminster. Now he has got a place at the National Film and Television School on a course to study composing for film. Strange, isn't it? she remarks, how things turn out. It looks like you and Paul will end up in the same business. Perhaps you'll end up working together…

There is a pause, and then Donna says, You and Paul were such friends, before Tommy died. He wanted to carry on being your friend. It was hard for him, losing Tommy and then losing your friendship too. He never had another friend like you at school. He's okay now. In fact he's got a lovely girlfriend who he's been going out with for a couple of years. She's a singer – in fact she's a classical singer, she sings opera. Who'd have thought Paul would end up with an opera singer?

She talks on like this, trying to fill the silence. At the mention of Tommy's name, something has happened to Ivan.

He has withdrawn, sunk into himself. Are you seeing anyone yourself? she asks finally.

No, he says.

There is a long silence. Donna takes a deep breath and says, Ivan, I know you blamed yourself for what happened to Tommy. But that's crazy. It's just as much Paul's fault, even mine. Paul's tortured himself about it too – if we hadn't been so wrapped up in that bloody music trophy, if we'd been looking out for Tommy, I mean at least you tried to stop him running out in to the road…

I didn't, Ivan says. I chased him out into the road. If I hadn't been there, he'd be alive. I killed him because I knew that was what was going to happen.

Donna closes her eyes. A tear squeezes out. She shakes her head and says, Ivan, why would you kill Tommy?

Because I knew it was going to happen.

Donna sits in silence for a long time, looking at the table. Then she gets up and says, I think you need help, Ivan. You should get help.

She leaves the pub. Ivan never hears from her again.

***

Soon after that Ivan starts having the dream. It appears only every few months to begin with, and then more and more frequently. The frequency accelerates the way the final sands in an hourglass seem to fall in a rush.

***

Cycling home one day, a nut hits Ivan on the nose.

***

He stands at the edge of the Tribal Village, looking up the row of tents. From a chestnut tree just the other side of the perimeter fence, two crows take off simultaneously and flap away across the countryside.

✳✳✳

He is sitting by the canal, turning Chronos's card over and over between his fingers. He stands up.

✳✳✳

"That's up to you," Chronos is saying. "When you first go back, you'll remember everything about the future. Then you'll start to forget. You must try not to forget. Only by remembering can you make things right."

✳✳✳

Paul's mum is talking with the teacher after the prize-giving. Everybody is laughing. They should not be laughing.

✳✳✳

The last grain of sand is tumbling down. Ivan is looking at it. He turns to Chronos and asks, "How many times have I been here before?"

Chronos smiles his condescending smile and nods towards the grain of sand. Ivan turns back to it. They seem to have all the time in the world.

"How many grains of sand are there in the universe?" says Chronos. "How many grains of sand are there in all the universes that could ever have existed?"

***

Ivan and Donna are throwing pebbles against a concrete breakwater, watching them accumulate. The falling pebbles sound an endless, brittle click. The sunlight off the sea is dazzling.

***

Tommy approaches the junction and seems to slow for a moment. Ivan, for a tiny fraction of a second, hesitates too. And then he remembers. The boy will die. He springs forward to save him.

***

The final grain of sand speeds towards the bottom of the hourglass. Ivan glances across and sees Chronos smile. The room fills with an alien laughter.

[This story is excerpted from a cycle of interconnected stories, *The Central Line*.]

At The Witching Hour

By Isabella Hunter

Leanne hovered in the hallway looking through the groups of students. She could happily slide into any one of them and not be out of place. However, that wasn't what she was after. What she wanted was more information. For that, she needed someone who was by themselves.

Ruby was alone, leaning against the wall, texting on her phone. She was one of the popular girls with long bleached blonde hair and tall compared to all the other girls in the year. Leanne walked over, taking the empty space next to her. "How are you doing?" Leanne asked.

Ruby's fingers hesitated over the keypad. There was a pause where neither of them talked. "I'm alright," she said finally, "I guess."

"You don't sound alright," Leanne said. "What's bothering you?" She took this opportunity to glimpse at Ruby's phone. She was texting someone, but the name had been changed to a nickname she didn't recognise. The content of the texts was what piqued Leanne's interest. The last text was from the other person. *'Have you tried talking to them yet?'* it read. Ruby hadn't replied, that was what she seemed to be procrastinating over.

Ruby bit her lip. "So there is someone I like but I'm not sure how to approach them," she said. Her eyes scanned the hallway, pausing for a moment on a girl named Charley.

If the person she liked was a girl that would explain her hesitation. Leanne had never known Ruby to struggle to get a boyfriend in the past but trying to find out if another girl was gay and interested would make it harder. "Do they know you like them?"

"We're friends but I haven't asked them if they want anything more than that," she said. "I was thinking of messaging The Witching Hour about it and seeing if they know if the person likes me."

"Doesn't it cost, though?" Leanne knew already that it cost to get information from The Witching Hour, but she didn't want Ruby paying to find out if Charley liked her.

"How about–"

"Come in, class," Mr. Garcia called.

The students filed into the class, moving to their respective seats. Leanne was at the end of a row in the middle. A few moments later, Nicholas came and sat next to her.

Nicholas had transferred to the school at the start of the year after his parents had moved from the city. They'd got themselves set up in a nice neighbourhood in a house that they owned outright. Nicholas was of average build, with short brown hair and hazel eyes. Even his grades were average: never top of the class but never bottom either. "Hey Leanne," he said, pulling out his maths book from his bag.

"How are you doing today, Nicholas?" Leanne smiled. He was the closest thing to a true friend she had in the school. She felt like everyone else's second choice, which made her perfect to share problems with because she wasn't involved. Leanne was an impartial witness for the students of the school.

Nicholas thumbed through his workbook. "I'm still feeling like an outsider in this school," he said. "I saw you talking with Ruby. You just get on with everyone. I wish I had your confidence."

"I just ended up getting to know everyone because people pay me to do their homework, and it spread from that."

Mr. Garcia cleared his voice. "If you could all turn to the section on quadratic equations." The room filled with the sound of pages being turned and the chatter died down. Mr. Garcia guided the class through the formula for solving the equations on the chalk board.

The class was then instructed to work through the questions on the handout. It was filled front and back with equations, going well into double digits. Quiet talking filled the class as everyone settled into their work. Leanne couldn't focus on the questions, though. Instead, she was watching Charley.

Charley was in the row ahead of her, sat with a group of her friends. Leanne didn't know if Charley was interested in girls, as any relationships she'd had weren't public. Her friends were a mix of girls and boys, with some in the higher year.

Leanne checked the back of the room where Ruby was sitting. She was tapping her worksheet with her pen, staring at the back of Charley's head. The guy next to her said something too quiet for Leanne to make out. Ruby responded with a one-word answer without turning towards him.

Leanne's phone buzzed in her pocket, making her jump. Her hand twitched to check the notification, but she resisted. The minute hand on the clock pointed to half past the hour. She debated trying to sneak a glance at her phone. Mr. Garcia was busy talking a student on the front row through a problem, but she knew he'd look over the second she pulled out her phone. She scanned the class. She glanced around at her classmates. She couldn't let any of them see her messages either.

"Hey, Leanne, can I get your opinion on something?" Nicholas asked in a hushed voice.

"Go on."

Nicholas ran a hand through his messy hair, taking in a deep breath. "I think a girl likes me," he said.

Leanne's heart started pounding. She hadn't considered that anyone else would be interested in him. She took a deep breath to calm herself. "What makes you say that?" she asked.

"It's just the little things, y'know? She's talking to me a lot more, texting and stuff as well. I don't know, maybe I'm reading too much into this."

"Are you interested in her?" Leanne asked. "It doesn't matter how she feels if you're not interested in her."

"I don't know. I had to cut off a relationship when I transferred and I'm not entirely sure I'm over it yet. I guess I'll see what happens. It isn't like she's asked me out or anything yet."

"I guess that's true."

"Who knows? Maybe she just wants to be friends," Nicholas said. He let out a half-hearted laugh.

"I'll be back in five," she told Nicholas. Leanne stood up, grabbing her bag. "I'm going to the bathroom, Mr. Garcia," she called across the room, walking towards the door.

She closed the door behind her, making her way through the empty halls. It was peaceful without any other students rushing around jostling her with their bags. She needed some time to think.

The bathroom floors and walls were covered in cream tiles. A thin layer of water covered the floor from where a girl had blocked a sink with toilet roll and left the tap on. All the stalls were vacant. Leanne went to the cubicle farthest away from the door.

Graffiti was scrawled on every spare inch of the walls and door. Declarations of love and friendship. Others were snide remarks about other students. Anyone and anything was fair game on these walls. Then, in clear handwriting was '@

TheWltchingHour for all your wishes and curses'. It was clear from the girl's handwriting that the first 'I' had been replaced with an 'L' making it easier to find the correct account.

Leanne pulled her phone from her pocket and unlocked it. Notifications flooded the screen, scrolling the next off the screen. Over twenty messages had been sent to *TheWltchingHour* since she'd last checked it on lunch break, making this her busiest day yet. Most of them were simple requests, but it did mean she was likely to make a decent amount of money tonight.

One caught her eye though. It was from a girl called Danielle in Nicholas's German class. The message had been sent just before class had started, and she had already transferred the money to Leanne. *'Does Nicholas like anyone?'* the message read.

Leanne couldn't turn down this opportunity. She could get Danielle to back away from Nicholas by using her power via The Witching Hour. *'Nicholas isn't interested in anyone. He isn't over his last relationship yet.'* Leanne smiled to herself and tapped send.

She turned off notifications to stop the incessant buzzing, something she should have done earlier, but it meant she'd got to deal with Danielle. She returned to class and took her seat next to Nicholas again, continuing her work. The quadratic equations before her were simple enough but her attention kept drifting away from them.

She loved to people-watch. She even had a miniature notebook she used to record information about students. Each student had already found somewhere they belonged within the hierarchy of the school. The seating of the classroom reflected that as well, with the back row dominated by popular girls, including Ruby, all with long, perfectly styled hair. Next to them sat athletic, conventionally attractive boys. They were always the rowdiest, but a quick glare from Mr. Garcia usually settled them down again.

The rest of the room was a medley of smaller groups of tight-knit friends. Leanne knew the secrets and ties that connected everyone in the room to each other. The lies hidden beneath the surface.

Nicholas peered over at her worksheet, huffing when he saw she hadn't passed question three. Nicholas was the one person she didn't know much about. He had joined partway through the term and hardly interacted with anyone but her. She suspected the only reason he'd latched onto her was because she didn't have any particularly close friends.

After he'd made friends with her he hadn't tried with anyone else. Maybe it made his life easier being separated from the drama of a normal school life. But now there was Danielle vying for his attention, getting closer to him.

Leanne was jolted from her thoughts by the ringing of the school bell, signalling the end of class. "You're all free to go," Mr. Garcia called. "Just leave your worksheets on the desks."

Leanne cursed when she looked at her barely started sheet. She tucked her pen into her pocket and grabbed her bag. She headed towards the door. Nicholas jogged up behind her, weaving in and out of the other students. "I'll walk home with you," he said.

The halls filled with students. Some were rushing to get out while others clogged up the hallway by milling around in large groups. Someone caught Leanne's eye, standing motionless at the end of the corridor. It was Danielle.

Her face brightened when she saw Nicholas walking in her direction. She only cast a cursory glance in Leanne's direction. Danielle came up to Nicholas. "Nicky, I want to ask you something," she said.

"No worries. What is it?" Nicholas's voice was as friendly as ever, but Leanne noticed a slight stiffness to his stance.

"Can we talk in private?" Danielle cast a glance over at

Leanne.

"Uhh, sure," he said. "Hey, Leanne, I'll be back in a minute. Just wait by the gates for me, okay?"

Danielle was heading towards a quieter hallway. Nicholas smiled and waved to Leanne as he followed Danielle. Leanne watched them disappear around the corner. She knew what Danielle was about to do. She was going to confess, ignoring what Leanne had said to her through The Witching Hour.

Leanne rushed through the students. She needed to be outside. She needed to get away from the maelstrom of chatter and general laughter. Once she got out into the front courtyard, it wasn't as claustrophobic anymore. She took a breath of fresh air, allowing the early autumn sun to warm her. She leaned against the wall, counting the students as they left the gate.

"I'm back," Nicholas said as he joined her. "Let's get going."

Leanne pushed off from the wall, following him out of the school gates. She cast a glance around the courtyard, looking for Danielle. Leanne saw her standing by the front entrance, arms crossed over her chest, watching them in turn.

"What are you plans for tonight, then?" he asked.

Leanne blurted the first thing that popped into her head. "I'm doing homework tonight," she said.

"What homework do you have to do today?"

Leanne racked her brain for an answer. She had finished everyone else's homework, but she couldn't say she was just working through the backlog of requests to *TheWItchingHour*. "It's French homework," she said. She hadn't got round to it as of yet, so it wasn't a lie, but she intended to do that in the morning. It was also one of the classes that they weren't in together as Nicholas had been put into German instead.

"I won't be able to help you with that anyway, then." They turned off the main road and into the residential area where Leanne lived. The streets were lined with trees, their leaves tinged with orange and red at the edges. Houses were set back from the path, with long well-maintained gardens filled with late blooming flowers.

"Don't worry about it. I'll probably get it done in no time at all, but then mum will need help around the house."

They walked in silence for a minute. A lump had formed in Leanne's throat. She wanted to ask about Danielle but didn't know how to brooch the subject. To her right Nicholas let out a long sigh. "It turns out I was right," he said.

"What about?"

"The girl who asked to talk to me. She was the one I thought liked me."

"Danielle, the one from your German class?" Leanne asked, feigning innocence.

"Yeah, she asked me out." A red hue had tinged his cheeks. "I said no. Maybe in the future I might think about it but for now I just want to relax."

"It's probably for the best you don't rush into things." The knot in her chest loosened. She could keep Nicholas close to her for a little longer. Leanne's house came into view at the end of the street. It was half shaded by the large hazel tree which grew in the front garden. "But if you want to talk more, I'll be online tonight. Otherwise I'll see you tomorrow."

"Alright, then. Thanks for listening to me today, Leanne. It means a lot. I'll see you tomorrow." He waved before jogging across the road in the direction of his home.

Leanne sighed and let the tension ease from her shoulders. The gate squealed as she pushed it open. The garden was overgrown from neglect. Her mum was too busy to look after the garden, working two jobs to make ends meet.

She unlocked the front door and opened it. The living room was dark and empty, but the light from the kitchen was enough to see by to make her way through the house. Her mum's voice echoed ahead.

Leanne entered the kitchen. Her mum was sitting on a stool by the breakfast bar, phone clutched between her ear and shoulder, scribbling notes in a diary. "So Danielle is having a party tomorrow," she said, "and you want me around ten in the morning on the Saturday to do a full clean?"

Leanne couldn't make out the other half of the conversation but it had to be one of Danielle's parents. "At ten pounds an hour. The job will take about four hours. How does forty pounds sound to you?" Her mum wrote the figure down on a list entitled 'Credit Card', but the amount didn't bring it back into the positive.

Leanne's mum nodded along to whatever Danielle's parent was saying to her. "My daughter is home now so I have to go," she said, "but I have you booked in for Saturday so I'll see you then." She hung up, placing the phone down next to the piles of papers.

"Hey mum," Leanne said, pulling herself onto the other stool. She scanned the finance notebook her mum kept. It was upside down from where she was, but she could see the red ink of all their debts.

Her mum shut the book and tidied up the papers. "I'm sorry but I haven't had time to make you tea today, so grab a ready-meal out of the freezer."

"Why don't we make something together now?" Leanne knew she should get on with her requests for The Witching Hour, but opportunities to spend time with her mum were few and far between.

Her mum's mouth twisted into a sad smile. "I'd love to but I have another job to do tonight. I'll be home later though, chicken."

"No worries," Leanne said. Her chest tightened and tears pricked at the corners of her eyes. She turned her head away from her mum, hopping down off the stool.

"How about Saturday?" her mum suggested. "After I finish at Danielle's place we can cook together and have a movie night?"

"That sounds nice," Leanne replied. She left the kitchen, heading towards her bedroom. The stairs were silent even as she climbed them up to her room. She didn't bother with the main light, instead popping her desk lamp on. The sound of the front door going as her mum left reverberated around the house.

Her room was basic, with white walls and beech wood furnishings. Just the bare essentials. The only place she'd been able to express herself was with her bedding. She'd got it on a shopping trip before her dad had died. It was a midnight blue with stars speckled across it, particular constellations picked out brightly. Her parents had intended to live here happily forever and ever, but then her dad had died and her mum had been left with a mortgage meant for two working adults. So they couldn't afford more than minimalist decorations.

Leanne switched on her laptop. The blue glow filled the room during the start-up before dying down to a more subdued light. She typed in her password and opened a spreadsheet, checking it through to make sure she had completed, returned, and been paid for the homework she had done for her classmates.

Next, she opened *TheWltchingHour* on her browser. The number of messages hadn't exceeded thirty since she'd last checked. She started from the oldest one first. It was from Charley, the girl Ruby had been paying attention too. '*I have a feeling, but I wanted to know if Ruby likes me? As more than a friend?*'

Ruby had essentially confirmed this earlier with how she'd been acting. This was interesting as the two of them didn't interact all that much. Leanne unlocked her desk draw, pulled out her notebook and grabbed her mini notebook for comparison. Every student in the school was featured, with an ever growing compilation of information she knew about them. First she flicked to Charley's page and added a note about her suspicion on Ruby. Next she went over to Ruby to check what information was on her.

She didn't have anything directly from Ruby that substantiated it. However, other close friends had given Leanne information about it. She knew that Ruby was gay, and at least a few others had mentioned Charley, believing Ruby was crushing on her. Plus, with the way Ruby had been acting, it did seem possible it was Charley.

Leanne sighed. There were two ways this could go. It could result in a relationship between the two, but she didn't know if Charley was gay. It could ruin any form of friendship the two had grown to have though. Ruby had told her she wanted to approach them about it, so she was doing her a favour. She steeled her resolve and responded. *'To gain this knowledge from me will cost you £10'* Leanne sent back to Charley.

She moved onto the next requests. This one was simpler. All she had to do was go onto a beauty blog and comment with some inflammatory stuff. This one was almost like a running order. Leanne opened her banking and found the request to receive £10, she accepted and got to work on the beauty blog. Generally, after about three comments the account would get banned, but that was why she used temporary email addresses that stopped working after thirty minutes.

Leanne worked through her requests. She did refuse some that pushed things too far, such as requests to DDOS people, or spread lies about students or teachers. She also wouldn't give out personal information such as contact details or addresses. She wouldn't do anything that might end up getting her mum into trouble.

A message from Charley came through. *'Payment has been*

made.' Leanne checked her banking and saw it had come through.

'*I can confirm that Ruby is gay. Several sources suggest she does like you. However, this I do not know for certain.*' She clicked return and sent the message off. She would have to watch how this played out carefully.

Her screen flashed. A new message had come through, but it was a handle that she'd never seen before: *@Remy.* '*What is Leanne doing tonight?*' the message read. Leanne's hands shook over her mouse and blood pounded in her ears. This was the first time anyone had asked about her, and she had no idea who was behind the message.

Why did they want this information? Did they know she was behind *@TheWltchingHour*? No, that was impossible. There was nothing that could link her back to this.

Leanne searched through their profile. There was no profile picture, nothing on their timeline, and they didn't even have any followers, which was surprising, although they were following a lot of people. Leanne scrolled through the list: almost the entire school was on there. It was probably a safe bet they went to her school as well. But there was no-one in the school with a name even similar to Remy. Leanne checked other sites but there were no similar accounts.

She could refuse the request, but with something as basic as this it might create some suspicion about her. At the same time, she had to think of something to tell them. She couldn't say what she was actually doing. She resigned herself to answering them. '*This information will cost you £5*' she sent over. The pay wall might discourage them from pursuing this further.

Immediately another response came through. '*Alright.*' Leanne sighed and sent over her payment details. The payment came through within seconds of her sending the message. Maybe if it had been set at a higher amount they would have declined. Or at least hesitated.

Her fingers hovered over the keyboard. Now she needed to come up with something to say. Leanne tapped her finger on the desk with increasing ferocity. She could have just stated she didn't know what any one person would be doing at a particular time. She did have the safe option of what most people in the school believed she would be doing. '*Leanne is working through people's homework tonight.*'

With that she signed off from her laptop and worked through her French homework. The front door clicked as Leanne's mum returned from work. Leanne got up and ran downstairs to greet her. Her mum looked tired. Stray hairs had fallen out of her bun and her make-up could not hide the signs of fatigue. "Leanne, what are you doing up still?"

"I was working, doing people's homework, and look!" Leanne raised her phone to show the screen to her mum. "I made seventy pounds tonight. I'll send it over to you now." Her fingers were already flying across her phone screen.

"You really have made a lot. Will you not get in trouble for this?"

"I'm just doing homework," Leanne said, shrugging.

"Look, keep some for yourself," her mum said. "How about twenty pounds?"

"Are you sure? You work so hard and I want you to be able to have a break. That way, we can spend more time together."

"You do more than enough for me already," she said. She pulled Leanne into a tight hug, resting her head on top of Leanne's hair. "You're such a good girl, the best daughter a mother could ask for."

***

Light was streaming in through Leanne's window when she woke up, setting off an alarm bell in her head. She rolled over and checked her phone, swiping away the new notifications. It was half eight! She jumped out of bed and threw her uniform on. Cursing, she pulled her school stuff together. It was only half an hour until class – she wouldn't have time for any breakfast.

Her mum had gone for the morning, leaving a note about a ready-meal in the freezer for tea. Leanne's lunch box was resting on the corner of the note, filled with a plain ham sandwich and a breakfast bar. Leanne stuffed it into her school bag and hurried out.

She walked as fast as she could go without breaking into a jog. She came up to the school gates with ten minutes to spare. Luckily, first-period French was close by the front entrance. Rushing over, she found most the class were already waiting outside.

A classmate moved past her, settling against the wall next to her. Leanne glanced up. It was Dominic, a guy who settled nicely into the middle of the pecking order, not a loner but not in the upper echelons. He was one of Charley's close friends.

"Can you help me with my homework?" he asked.

"You know I charge for that, right? It's five pounds for one sheet."

"I only have three pounds on me," he said. "Look, we're running out of time." He looked down the corridor for any sign the teacher was coming.

"I'll do it this one time. If you ever ask again it'll be five pounds." Leanne pulled out her homework and handed it to Dominic. He scribbled down the answers onto his own sheet.

"Thanks, Leanne," he said, handing over his money. Dominic moved away and back towards his friends, including Charley, who were gathered on the other side of the corridor.

Miss Beaumont approached from the direction of the teachers' office. "Line up," she said. Her eyes looked tired and she clutched her coffee cup with both hands. Leanne was jostled around as everyone who wasn't already against the wall forced themselves into a single-file line. It curled from the classroom door all the way around the corner. Miss Beaumont took another sip of her coffee, waiting for silence.

She nodded in satisfaction and unlocked the classroom. There was no formal seating plan, but people are creatures of habit. Leanne moved to her usual seat at the back of the room. The French class was organised in single tables in four rows running down the room all facing the front.

Miss Beaumont believed it created a more productive study environment. In reality it meant those at the front were under close supervision but those at the back were free to do as they pleased. This was the one class where Leanne felt confident that she could respond to messages even during class.

Leanne waited for Miss Beaumont to finish setting up the class. Once the woman had settled behind her desk, nursing her coffee, Leanne pulled out her phone. It was a quiet start to the day compared to yesterday, with only a few requests. A new one had come through from @Remy. Curiosity got the better of her and she opened it. '*Does Leanne like anyone?*'

She smiled to herself. Whoever Remy was, they seemed to have a crush on her, which would be a first. The message had been sent before classes started, suggesting they were a student? Not that Leanne even had any idea if it was a boy or a girl behind their moniker. She sent off the payment request and waited.

Leanne worked through the other requests that she could get done during the lesson. For the ones she couldn't do until she got home, she messaged the senders to wait until the evening. Leanne emptied her inbox. There had been no reply from @Remy as yet. She placed the phone on her leg and turned her attention to her French work.

The rest of the class was uneventful. Leanne kept an eye on Charley and Ruby, watching for any sign that Charley was taking action based on what she'd said. She spied the two passing a sheet of paper between their tables. Leanne couldn't see anything of what was written on it, but their body language seemed relaxed.

Miss Beaumont collected up the homework at the end of the class. Dominic shot a thumbs up to Leanne after Miss Beaumont grabbed his sheet. She dismissed the class once everyone's work had been collected. Dominic waited for Leanne by his desk.

"Thanks for helping me out with that, Leanne."

"No worries." Leanne was watching Charley and Ruby, who were leaving the class together. "I didn't realise Charley was close friends with Ruby." She nodded towards the pair as they rounded the corner.

"Yeah, Charley said they really hit it off last night over messenger."

"That really came out of the blue," Leanne said.

"Nah, Charley has looked up to Ruby for a while."

"Oh, I didn't know that. Anyway, I'll see you round."

Nicholas was waiting in the hallway for her, as he usually did, so they could walk to the next class together. Her phone buzzed in her pocket but she ignored it, waving at Nicholas as she got to him.

Danielle appeared behind him from out of the crowd. "Hey, Nicky, I'm having a party tonight. You're going to come, right?" she asked. If she'd been affected by the rejection yesterday, there was no sign of it now.

"Who's going?" Nicholas asked.

"My friends, their friends, anyone one popular really."

"Sure, that sounds fun."

Danielle made eye contact with Leanne for the first time

since she'd come over. "I guess you can come as well, Leanne." Danielle was smiling but Leanne's chest was tight. She hadn't been invited to a party before. She didn't even have many nice clothes to wear.

"Thank you for the invite," Leanne said. "I have a lot of work to do tonight. But if I can finish it up fast enough I'll definitely come."

"Alright." Danielle moved away down the corridor.

Leanne and Nicholas watched in silence until she was out of sight.

"I hope you can make it," Nicholas said, "I'd rather not go alone."

"I'll see. Honestly, I'm not too sure it's my scene. Go on to class without me. I need to head to the bathroom." Leanne waved, turning off in the direction of the toilets. Her fingers itched to check the message that had come through.

The girl's bathroom was filled with other students. As soon as a cubicle became free, she darted in. She'd hardly shut the door before she had her phone unlocked. The payment had come through from @*Remy*. Leanne had made up her mind about what she was going to say.

'Leanne has no interest in anyone.'

She went to lock her phone when it came up that @*Remy* was typing. Unless they had another question for her, Leanne couldn't think why they would be responding. Her finger hovered over the lock button, waiting for @*Remy* to finish the message.

'I think we both know that is a lie.'

Leanne reread the sentence. No one had argued with her information before. No one knew she liked Nicholas.

Her phone shook in her hand. She locked it and slid it back into her pocket. Sinking down onto the toilet seat, she took deep breaths. Her pulse slowed with each exhale. Of course some people weren't going to be happy with what she told them. She decided not to not respond to the message and instead get on with her day.

***

Leanne couldn't concentrate in any of her next classes. She couldn't tell if @Remy knew that she was behind The Witching Hour or whether it was a coincidence that they were showing an interest in her.

Nicholas nattered on next to her, unperturbed by Leanne's one-word answers. Any thoughts about attending Danielle's party had been pushed from her mind. She had no idea who this person was and she didn't like that. New messages kept coming through to The Witching Hour, but Leanne was only looking for any from @Remy.

The lunch bell suddenly rang out, making her jump. She followed Nicholas through the corridor to their usual lunch spot. It was a small alcove off the main dining hall that still let them see out over the rest of the room. She liked to watch others interacting during lunch break.

Leanne settled down on the floor, pulling her lunch out of her bag. Nicholas bought his lunch from the canteen, giving her a few minutes to herself. Her thoughts were too scattered to deal with any of the requests she had. Instead, Leanne browsed her personal account, distracting herself with pictures of everyone's pets.

A notification covered the top of her screen. It was from @Remy. Leanne hesitated. She could ignore it and carry on with her day. She didn't need to know what they had to say to her. Leanne swiped it off the screen and continued looking at her timeline. Another notification came through.

Leanne tapped it this time. @TheWItchingHour came up with two new messages from @Remy.

'I know who you are. I expect to see you at the party tonight.'

'Otherwise, Nicky will find out exactly what you have been up to.'

Leanne felt the blood rushing to her face. Her fingers were numb and clumsy. Nicholas returned with a pasta pot. Leanne dropped her phone and the screen cracked! With a yelp of distress, she snatched her phone away from Nicholas and cradled it to her chest.

"You okay there, Leanne?"

"Yeah, it was a spider video," she lied, with a forced chuckle. "Gave me a bit of a shock is all."

Leanne hid her phone in her bag as Nicholas sat down next to her. His gaze searched her face. "Is your phone alright?" he asked. "It sounded like it cracked."

"It's fine, really." Leanne could hear the desperation in her voice. She hadn't had time to check the damage, to see if it was stuck on the messages from *@Remy*. "I've decided I'm going to the party though. I have all weekend to do work."

"Great, I can't wait." He perked up like a puppy about to go for a walk. "I can pick you up at seven," he said.

"Yeah, that's fine."

✳✳✳

Leanne's mum wasn't home when she got in from school. There was a note on the table about tea being in the fridge. Leanne pulled out her phone and texted her mum. *I'm going to the party at Danielle's tonight. Nicholas is taking me there and I'll be back before midnight x'*

Leanne had had no intention of going to the party until *@Remy* had messaged her about Nicholas. Now she had to go and confront *@Remy*, if she could find out who it was. Her first job, though, was to find something to wear.

Leanne didn't have any good outfits for a party, so she went to her mum's room. It was minimalist, like Leanne's, with a plain wardrobe next to the bed. Opening the door, Leanne rifled through the dresses, half of which she had never seen her mum wear before. She stopped at a black shift dress. She pulled it out, slipped it on, and surveyed herself in the mirror. The garment hung off her frame. Leanne grabbed a thin belt and cinched the dress at the waist.

The reflection showed her a child in an adult's clothes. Of course it did. She moved to her mum's make-up box. She added some mascara to her eyelashes and a dark red tint to her lips. Something to make her look more mature, more like the other girls who would be there.

By the time Leanne had got together everything she needed it was almost seven. A text came through from Nicholas: *'I'm just coming round the corner now. See you in five."*

'I'll come out now.'

Leanne grabbed her satchel and went downstairs. By the time she had got to the front door she could already see Nicholas walking towards her house. He was in blue jeans and a faded grey top. It was a stark contrast to the shirt and pants she saw him in everyday at school.

She opened the door and waved. Heat rose to her cheeks as she became aware of how different she looked compared to her uniform. She wore trousers to school so, even with tights on, her legs felt bare.

Nicholas didn't show any obvious reaction to her outfit. He just waved and waited by the gate for Leanne to come to him. "I know where Danielle's house is," he said as she approached. "It's just a short walk away."

There hadn't been any new messages from *@Remy* since the ones that had come through at lunch. A knot had formed in Leanne's stomach thinking about the party. She wished she had some inkling as to who *@Remy* was. A chill ran down her spine. It could be anyone, even Nicholas.

He was relaxed, his arms swinging by his sides, walking a touch in front of her. "What's up, Leanne? Why are you glaring at me?" He smiled back at her, causing all her doubts to disappear.

She took a deep breath, letting the muscles in her face relax. "I'm sorry," she said. "I think I'm just so nervous, and you look so calm."

"I definitely wouldn't be this calm if I didn't have you with me," he answered. "This is her house coming up on the left." He pointed to a large detached house. The lights were on in every window and the dull hum of music came from the building. Nicholas held open the gate, letting her through before following.

The curtains were drawn, the silhouettes of party-goers moving across them. Leanne checked her phone. They were only twenty minutes later than the start but the party already looked busy. As she came closer to the door the voices of the guests inside drifted towards them.

Leanne knocked on the door loud enough to be heard above the music. The door swung open to reveal Dominic. He beckoned Leanne and Nicholas into the house. "It's Nick and Leanne," he called.

"I'll come over in a second," Danielle responded from somewhere deeper in the house. Leanne couldn't see her from the entranceway. Directly ahead of the front door was a set of stairs leading up to a dark landing. To the right was a bright living room packed with people.

Leanne recognised different people from her year and even some from the year below them. Danielle came into the hallway. She was dressed in a sequinned dress with a full face of make-up that wouldn't have been out of place on the cover of vogue. "Oh, Nicky, I'm so happy you're here." She went straight in for a hug, wrapping her arms around his chest. "Leanne, you made it too. Fantastic."

Danielle led them through into the main room where everyone was gathered. It was an open plan living room come dining area. There was a table laid out with nibbles and drinks. People looked up from their conversations as Leanne followed Danielle into the living room.

Dominic had moved over to a group of guys he hung around with. Even Charley and Ruby were already sat next to each other on the couch. Leanne looked around the faces. Everyone seemed friendly towards her, but Leanne knew that she had affected everyone's life in this room. Not always for the better.

Danielle tapped her phone and the music stopped. Everyone's conversations died away. "Everyone, I'd like your attention!". All the guests turned to face her. "I'd like to present our guest of honour." People's faces were a mix of curiosity and confusion. They looked between Leanne and Nicholas.

Nicholas leaned down to Leanne's ear, whispering, "Do you know what she's talking about?"

"I should go," Leanne said. She shuffled her feet backwards but couldn't bring herself to turn and leave.

Danielle locked eyes with Leanne, and Leanne flinched. "Probably the most renowned person in our school has joined us. Who knew that The Witching Hour was unassuming, little Leanne?" Danielle announced.

Everyone was staring at her. They whispered to each other. Her skin itched. Nicholas's eyes were on her too. She felt sick.

"Is it true?" he asked.

Tears stung her eyes. "I was just trying to make some money," she tried to explain. "I was trying to help out my mum."

"You don't have the right to spread our secrets!" a girl called from the back of the room.

"I'm just doing what you guys ask of me. You pay me to do this. I only tell people what I'm asked, never more than that. If you want to blame anyone, blame each other!" Leanne shoved

Nicholas out the way and ran out the door.

Tears streaked down Leanne's face as she ran back in the direction of her house. One of her heeled shoes turned her ankle over and she cried out in pain. She pushed through the gate and limped to the front door. She fumbled to get her keys into the lock.

The house was dark and quiet. The note from Leanne's mum was still on the table where she'd left it. According to the clock on the wall it wasn't even eight. Her phone had been buzzing incessantly.

She hesitated. It could be anyone messaging her. It could be Nicholas. Leanne winced, remembering how he'd looked at her... before she'd run away. That's what she had done. Run away from her problems. She pulled out her phone.

Notification after notification scrolled across her lock screen. Some were to *@TheWltchingHour*, others to her personal account. It was a blur of names and monikers that she knew. Leanne unlocked her phone, ignoring the abuse being hurled at her private account, and switched to *@TheWltchingHour*.

The inbox had blown up with messages. Even conversations that were long since dealt with had fresh messages coming through. Leanne wrote an announcement and pinned it to the top of her account.

The Witching Hour is closed to requests at this time.

Leanne froze the account, stopping any more messages coming through to her. She was left with her personal account, which had messages and comments flooding in on every post. Nicholas had texted her several times since she'd left the party.

'Where did you go?'

'Please respond when you get this so I know you're okay.'

'I don't care what Danielle said. When you left she came over and told me that she had messaged @TheWltchingHour and what you'd told her. I don't like what you told her, but the outcome would have been the same

either way. You're still my friend and I care about you.'

Leanne stared down at the messages. A sent receipt would be visible to Nicholas. He'd know that she'd opened them. *'I'm sorry I went home. I'm safe.'* Leanne muted the conversation. She sat in silence, watching the notifications scroll over her screen.

Footsteps broke the silence as someone approached the front door. Keys jingled as the person unlocked the door. Leanne's mum entered, kicking off her shoes in the hallway. Her eyebrows knitted together when she saw Leanne sat at the breakfast bar.

"Honey, what's up? Weren't you meant to be at a party tonight?"

"I decided to call it early."

A bright smile spread across her mum's face and Leanne couldn't help smiling in response. "I have some microwave popcorn in the cupboard," she said. She was already rooting through the various packets and tins. Her mum lifted out a battered pack of popcorn. "Go find a movie for us to stream and I'll make hot chocolate. We'll start our mother-daughter bonding day early."

"Alright," Leanne nodded. She put the TV on and pulled the blanket out of the storage cushion. Leanne's phone flashed next to her with a new notification. It was Ruby. She opened the message.

'Charley let me know that she messaged you through @ TheWltchingHour and that is what gave her the courage to talk to me. We have decided to start dating, although not publicly. Just taking things slow. I wanted to let you know because even though everyone is saying what you did was bad, for me it has been great. So I guess what I'm saying is thanks, Leanne.'

Leanne's mum plopped down on the sofa next to her, placing the bowl of warm, buttery popcorn between them. Leanne pressed play on the controller, starting the movie.

The Witch of Soneton

By A J Dalton

They wouldn't leave her alone. No matter where she went, someone eventually found her. She'd retreated into the remotest parts of the forest, where the impassable thickets, the closeness of the trees and the darkness beneath the canopy should have meant she remained undisturbed. Yet hopelessly lost travellers, perhaps guided by mischievous gods, had still stumbled across her simple dwelling. Or far-ranging hunters had been led to her by deer, boar or other game seeking refuge. Or the lovesick determined on begging a potion of her would find their way to her door. Or, worst of all, the Witchfinders would not rest until her hiding place had been uncovered.

The world – be it the whim of nature, the wilfulness of humankind, or the decree of divine intervention – insisted that she continue to accommodate, indulge and ultimately serve it. Perhaps it was just the price any being had to pay for their existence. Or it was the particular price paid by those who dared dabble in what the ignorant called magic. Or she had somehow been individually cursed. Whichever it was, a power far greater than herself had long ago decided she should never know peace.

She'd tried putting up totems of forbiddance and warning in the forest around her home but, if anything, these had simply served as sign-posts to those intent on their own need. She'd tried using wards, spells of concealment and mazing magicks, but these had only attracted power-hungry demons, fed malign imps and caused her more trouble than if she'd never used them in the first place. And, besides, they seemed ineffective in deterring those with the blind faith and zealous fervour of Witchfinders. Finally, she'd tried fleeing to precipitous crags, sucking swamps and the most inhospitable fastnesses. Yet still they'd found her.

Always something was demanded of her. They begged her rarest ingredients and ministrations, ingredients she needed to sustain herself but did not have the heart to deny them. They sought her wisdom and foresight, uncaring of her sacrifice and the toll it took. And the Witchfinders wanted her life and very soul from her.

She was amazed that there was anything left of her, so long and so much had she been forced to yield. Wasn't it enough? Would it ever be enough? Of course not. Only her total capitulation would satisfy the Witchfinders. No matter how many of them she undid or sent running for the hills, there would always be another coming for her a few months later. No matter whether she was ruthless or merciful with them, they kept coming. No matter whether she warned them, displayed the sort of strength to make them think better of their actions or pleaded reason, still they came.

She was so tired. So very tired. She was being worn down and the Witchfinders seemed stronger and stronger. That, or they were becoming all too familiar with her tricks, habits and weaknesses.

The last one had so nearly caught her out. If her fox-familiar, Greynard, hadn't detected the man's scent upon the trap and warned her, she would never have noticed it hidden beneath the leaf-litter there down by the stream where she collected water every day. Its iron teeth would have snapped shut upon her legs, breaking bones and poisoning or disrupting her magic with its tang, will-craft and malign intention. She would have lain broken and in defenceless agony awaiting his approach and killing stroke.

Oh, but he'd been a wily one. He'd known to keep by the running water, as that masked his presence from her senses. He must have spied upon her for a number of days in order to learn her daily route down to the side-pool. He knew better than to confront her directly. And, when she avoided the trap, he loosed an iron-tipped arrow from cover.

She desperately sought to *move* air, to take the lethal dart from its course, but little more than a breeze ever made it down beneath the trees. At the last, she called for the rock where she usually sat to become a lodestone, and that dragged the arrow downwards, away from her heart at least. The arrow reached her, pierced the lower section of her gathering robe, shot between her legs and struck the ground just behind her.

Terrified, she flung herself down. She touched the wooden shaft. *Return you to the bow and heart that have you as their killing part!* The quarrel twitched and shook, came free and went whistling back across the stream.

There was no scream. Only taut silence. He had to be wearing armour, or have some other form of protection, like verses from his holy book pinned to his chest. She rolled awkwardly behind her sitting stone, praying to any power that cared that she no longer presented him with a target. She would have cast a confusion spell, but she did not have his precise location, and knew the running waters of the stream would dissipate much of the magic in any event. She dared not move, but knew he could be coming closer with every second that passed.

She risked peeking out. Sure enough, a shadow was moving stealthily between the trees. The stream would give him no trouble and then he'd be right on top of her. She ducked down. What to do? *Think. Be calm, like a cloud floating on high.* But she was no cloud. She was here grovelling in the earth and he was only moments away. *Like a flower nodding on a hazy day.* But she was no bloom enjoying a summer's day – she was at the end of her season, withered and now failing.

He called out. 'Show yourself, mab. In the name of God, I command you.' His voice was measured and pitiless. His weapon would already be trained on her location.

He had not crossed the stream, though. He was wary, and that was probably the only reason she was still alive. He feared her in some way, and she had to play on that. 'Your god is new to this land, no? By what right does you god command, then?' she croaked, not having spoken aloud in many moons.

'Blasphemous wretch! God created this world. He is eternal and always has been.'

'He's male? Ha! Why am I not surprised? What does he want with a poor old woman minding her own business off in the woods, eh? Why does he have to send some unfortunate fellow like you? Why can't he come see me himself? Is he afraid? Is he not so high and mighty after all?'

'God is not answerable to one as lowly as you, twisting demon. Step out and meet his judgement.'

'Why? I have done neither him nor you any ill.'

'You are a blight upon the forest and all who live within its proximity. The crops of Soneton are spoilt, milk turns in the udders of cattle, fruit rots on the vine, and the women are made barren. You muddle the minds of youth and adult alike, and our children are stolen from their beds!' He was losing his self-control, his self-possession. 'You are a living corruption!' he shouted.

'What madness is this you talk, man?' she called, her voice nowhere near as strong as his own. 'Women have many ways of not getting with child if they so choose. Trust me, if they've already born a man one or two children, then it is their own decision if they have no more. It is simple – they can avoid rutting at the time of month when they are in season, they can take a weak distillation of cowslip, and so forth. As for stealing children, what would I want with squalling brats? They're nothing but a trial. Or do you think I eat them?' She cackled at the silliness of it.

'Monster!' he railed, silencing the birdsong of the forest around them.

He was beyond listening to sense, that was clear. And his passions now had the better of him. She muttered words and the boar tattoo upon her thigh slipped free from beneath her robes. Its shadowy bulk grew until it was larger than the rock behind which she sheltered. It scraped the ground with a front hoof, lowered its tusks and then charged for the man. She made angry grunting noises to complete the illusion.

The hunter screamed and immediately released his arrow. It speared through the phantom, encountering no resistance, hit the ground and bounced off into the undergrowth. Now she stepped out to face him, as her familiar faded upon reaching the stream.

He met her eyes and gasped in horror. Apparently deciding he did not have time to nock and let fly with another arrow, he quickly discarded his bow and drew a short stabbing sword from a scabbard at his waist. She felt the cold menace and intention of the man-forged iron even from this distance.

'There is no need,' she pleaded, knowing her words would be in vain. She raised her hands palm up and spread them wide, to show she meant no harm.

He was already leaping across the stream and rushing straight at her. She cowered back, defenceless.

And the jaws of the Witchfinder's own trap closed upon

him, crushing his legs and biting deep into his flesh. He arched in agony and collapsed, crying out piteously.

She looked down at him. His hair was greying at the temples and thinning on top. His face was lined with years of care or worry, but the crow's feet at his eyes suggested he may also have known moments of laughter and happiness. His blue eyes were watery as he looked up at her in pain and panic. 'You are not as young as the others before you,' she considered. 'A man your age will not easily recover from such injuries, if at all. Your hunting days are over—'

'Have done, crone! I will not hear your taunts!' he choked. He looked for his blade, and moaned as he realised it was beyond his reach.

She crouched near him. 'You are bleeding a great deal. You will not last long. I can save you but—'

'Keep your filthy hands away from me!' he wheezed. 'You will not have my soul from me. I am not afraid to die.'

She sighed sadly. 'This is needless, man, but I will respect your wish.'

He mumbled prayers to his god, a god who had forced him to come here and lay the self-same trap that now killed him. Was the god simply cruel or amused by such irony? She could hardly fathom it.

***

She'd stayed with him until his lips had stopped moving and the breath no longer came from him. Then, with much effort, she'd dragged him, along with all his poisonous iron, back across the stream.

Such a shame that he'd refused to live. It would have been nice to have the company while she tended him back to health. Perhaps he would have wanted to stay with her beyond that.

They might have had some years of contentment together. She told herself she was just being a foolish old woman.

She'd arranged him neatly and covered him over with tree bark and fresh earth. His body would nourish the forest now, and through the forest something of him would live on. 'From death comes new life,' she spoke over the grave.

She could have used death magicks to keep him animated beyond the moment he had died. But such magicks were dangerous, particularly when the object of those magicks was unwilling. If the hunter had refused to be raised, then a dark spirit may have taken his place instead. She might have ended up making a far worse enemy for herself than she had already encountered.

***

It hadn't always been this way. There'd been a time when all the people of Soneton had valued her ointments, herb lore, nursing skills and far sight. Back when she'd still been comely and spry, they'd welcomed her into the town on market days so that she could tend to sickly cattle, troubled maids and those ailing in spirit. They often brought their grizzling children to her. She'd even been courted by one of the braver farmhands from the local area. What had his name been? He'd had blue eyes, a strong brow and jaw, and a gentle way about him. Garath, that was it. Sweet Garath.

All had been well and she'd known a measure of happiness. Until the priest had come – sent from the region's main town of Canterbree – with his black garb, strange learning, hard words and judging ways. The people had quickly come to fear Father Severin. There was talk of other towns being too slow to embrace the Church of Civilization and suffering serious reprisals from the Duke's standing force in Canterbree. It was said that several folk in the hamlet of Lourbrook had been hung for the unholy worship of animals. And that a wise woman over in Widford had been burnt alive for consorting with devils and casting curses upon the good people of that place. What was more, Father Severin set clever word-traps, was quick to find fault, had the role of communing directly with the new god on behalf of both the Duke and the wider people, and had the power of something called *divine blessing*.

Soneton had dutifully built a church and a house for its minister – though the town had hardly had the spare materials or hands for such work. Elder Corin had heartily agreed – for the good of his *immortal soul*, as well as everyone else's, of course – that the Father should immediately have a permanent seat on the Council. The new Council had then unanimously agreed that every newborn, marriage and burial needed to receive a priestly blessing if it was to be Council-recorded, within law or welcomed by the god. The rules had confused some of the townsfolk to begin with, but then everyone was told they need not work on the seventh day if they instead went to Church to hear Father Severin speak and explain things. That had made going to Church very popular among the farmhands, that was for sure, and neighbours got to meet neighbours, young people got to make friends, a certain amount of courting took place, and trade and business could be done. Everyone had ended up going, and they continued to do so even when the Council had decided all those living within the town should pay a tithe to the Church on the first day of every month.

Yes, everyone had ended up going... everyone except for her. She hadn't wanted to interfere or cause problems. Better to keep her own counsel. She'd always found it better to *live and let live*. If there were those who found the new god helpful and generous, then let them go to Church. Others would come to her, just as they always had, albeit that now they came more stealthily and at strange hours of the day and night.

Yet then Garath had come to her, his eyes and expression full of conflict and woe. She hadn't needed him to say anything, indeed she'd raised a hand to pre-empt his pained apology, tortured explanations and briar-bush declarations of continued love. She'd never struggled to read him. She *knew*. At least he had come to warn her: she still meant that much to him.

'They are on their way to arrest you,' he'd mumbled miserably as he'd watched her pack her most valuable items into a basket. 'Severin was speaking powerfully from the pulpit just now, in that way that he does. Pretty much all of them have now turned against you. Wouldn't be surprised if the whole town was on its way here.'

She'd nodded silently as she'd busied herself. When she was done, she gazed at him, working to fix his sweet face in her memory. Who knew when she would see him again? If ever? She'd given him a single kiss on the lips, and then she'd left.

How long ago had that been? A goodly while. Yes, he'd be dead by now. Poor Garath. She hoped he'd had a good life, or that he'd at least known a measure of happiness in the briefness of his human span.

***

The iron-grey sky pushed down upon the forest. It weighed heavily on all those within. She found that she could no longer stand comfortably straight beneath the constant pressure, and that she was developing a near permanent stoop. She wanted to scream with the relentless agony of it. What was happening?

She tasted cold metal in the air. A blade. No, blade*s*. Crossed to form a crucifix.

She trembled in fear. He was coming for her himself. And

he brought many iron-shod servants with him.

She knew that she wouldn't be able to stand against both his mind-dulling cant and their unforgiving weapons. And she was too old and bent to run any further.

This was the end, then. It would be a relief in some ways. Still, she hated to give him and his smug god any sort of satisfaction. She cursed them with everything she had… but still they came.

'May you be swallowed by the earth and then tree roots slowly, slowly pierce your flesh and guts. May they grow through you and feed upon your blood and fluids, allowing you just enough to stay alive, so that you are trapped, silently screaming mandrakes forever more.'

Yet, these men – with their axes, scythes, blades and fire – no longer feared the very nature that had first fed, raised and clothed them. They had turned away from a worship of that nature, to a worship of themselves and their Civilization, ripping down trees and tearing up the earth in order to construct altars and churches of self-glorification. And to prove they had no fear and would accept no challenge to their dominion, they had come at last in their full power to finish off her own kind once and for all.

For the last time, she looked around the clearing in which her simple dwelling stood. She'd lived in little more than a hovel, but it had been sheltered and snug, and more generous than she could ever have dared ask. Herbs, edible flowers and fungi grew all around, their delicate and wholesome fragrances revitalising to any who breathed them in. Spongey mosses, frilly ferns and lengths of bark provided more than enough for comfortable bedding. And ground water trickled along mazing courses and down a slight slope to a deep pool that was always cool and fresh. It would be a shame not to know this place again.

The forest stilled. The birds were silent, and the creatures beneath the leaf litter ceased their movement.

They were here. *He* was here.

She hobbled over to her sitting stone and lowered her creaking bones down. She was ready.

She did not have to wait even a breath or a heartbeat.

Severin stepped from amongst the trees directly ahead of her. Although she could not see or hear them, she scented the men sheathed in iron spacing themselves around the perimeter of the glade. Their *tang* was unmistakable.

His eyes were the flame and smoke of a smithy, his brow was an anvil and he held himself like a human-forged weapon. Around his neck was a heavy black chain with the great golden sign of his god attached to the end. He had hardly aged since her time in Soneton. His god had become strong over the years. How many had he sacrificed to win such power? And how many more did he still intend to sacrifice? Her, for one.

Severin's sneering slash of a mouth whispered its accusations: 'Demon!… Succubus!… Devourer of souls!… Murderer of children. Corruptor of innocence. She who would turn love into sexual perversion. Servant of sin! Agent of damnation! Unholy and hideous hag! Witch! I *name* you.'

'Bit of a mouthful, all that, isn't it?' she couldn't help replying.

'Your days of mocking and twisting all that's good in the world are over. No longer will you be permitted to plague God's world of men. Your forked tongue will be pulled out and cooked over a fire. Your entrails will be pulled from your still breathing body and used to strangle you.'

'I see. With chopped onions and garlic?' She smiled tiredly. Her heart really wasn't in it.

'Oh, Lord, protect us from the foul magicks and bewitchments of this—'

She sighed. 'Look, spare me all the speeches. Just get on with it.'

Severin stumbled over his words. His eyes went upwards, but the leaves and branches of the trees guarding the glade blocked his sight of the skies, even though he tottered forwards and craned his neck. 'Lord!' he yelled. 'Protect us from this she-devil. Our every word and action are a prayer to–'

'Spit it out, already!'

'–are... are... a beseechment that...'

'Beseechment isn't even a word. You'll tie your tongue in knots and choke if you aren't careful.'

He gagged. His eyes widened in horror and he clutched at his throat. 'Now! Kill her!' he croaked.

The brave and enraged battle-cries of the soldiers of Severin's god rose up around her. There were a dozen of them charging in from all directions, mighty swords raised on high, plate armour gleaming.

She closed her eyes. This was it, then. She'd fought as she could, but now she was done. She was out of tricks. She gave herself up to the forest, and the cosmos, reconciled. She was grateful for the life she'd led.

'Kill her!' shrieked Severin. 'Strike her down!'

She felt them closing in upon her.

'Do not hesitate! Stand up, good men.' His voice was querulous and hysterical with delight.

There were grunts of effort. They must be swinging their weapons down upon her right now. It seemed to take forever.

'What are you doing? No! Fight free. Trust in the Lord.'

She opened her eyes a peek. 'Oh dear. Oh. Come on, you can do it.'

Yet the weight of their armour had dragged them down into the wet ground. Most were up to their knees already, and one was up to his waist, making shrill cries of fright. Severin staggered forwards in an attempt to free the nearest one, but the priest was a big man, and he was soon sunk up to his calf muscles.

'That chain of yours is dragging you down,' she advised him. 'Throw it off before it's too late.'

His eyes blazed and he spat his hatred. 'Give up the sign of God? Renounce him? In the moment of true testing? I think not, you fiend. I know what game it is you play.'

She shook her head. 'Do you not see he has forsaken you? Perhaps he does not approve of this attempt at murder. Perhaps he disapproves of all you have done in his name. Or perhaps he never existed in the first place.'

'Foul blasphemer! Stop your ears against her poison, men!'

'Some of them are already beyond hearing, I fear. Will you not listen? Or see with your own eyes that it is only your own foolish vanity that is preventing you from saving yourself?'

***

She'd had to give up her home, what with all the iron sunk into the ground around it. Besides, Soneton was now unguarded and she fully intended to reacquaint herself with it, to reclaim it as her own. Finally, she would be free to feed upon its children once more. Their youth would become hers, and both her beauty and powers would be restored. How entirely delicious!

In the Shadow of Pendle

By Garry Coulthard

Francis Whittle was somewhere between pissed off and perplexed. The new guy, who had graduated from traffic school and relocated to Lancashire, had called him asking for his professional opinion. Which was annoying because he had been going home.

The new guy, Kinder, had been loitering down the backroads of Pendle looking for dickheads in high powered cars wearing Mr T chains and boots full of cocaine. He had come across something odd. On investigating further, he had decided that instead of calling in his findings to the station, which he should have done, he'd call Francis and ask him to come over and see what he thought. Francis had dutifully agreed, in an effort to at least appear helpful.

Another reason he was annoyed was that it was a full moon. Full moons always brought out the weirdos. Tree humpers, rapists, naked dancers, murderers, and such like. They all seemed to prefer a full moon. Francis reckoned that over eighty percent of his strangest collars had happened under a full moon. He hated working them. Tonight's moon was full, but with an unusual pink hue. Some kind of eclipse or solar storm, the weatherman had said. A once, or maybe twice, in a lifetime astrological phenomenon. Francis thought it would just bring out even more of the great unhinged.

***

When he arrived, Kinder came over to him and sheepishly pointed to the middle of the field behind him. Francis almost laughed in Kinder's face. In the field was a shadowy figure, half standing, half floating. A scarecrow. He looked Kinder directly in the eyes and asked him, in his most serious tone, if that was what he had summoned him for. Kinder nodded in the affirmative. He also tried to suggest that it had somehow been moving. That *somehow*, Francis assured him, was the wind running down the side of Pendle. He asked him if he'd ever seen a scarecrow before, chuckled and strode off to examine it, Kinder in tow.

As per his original assumption, it was a scarecrow, albeit it a rather convincing and quite macabre one. It had the appearance of a man who had become completely entwined in a tree, a silver birch, he thought. His papier-mâché face, which looked quite realistic, had its mouth sewn shut with the tiniest of little silver branches. Others were woven throughout its face and nose. Oddly, Francis noticed, it had closed eyelids – why make such a scarecrow? So interweaved were the branches that they had got twisted with its clothes, giving the impression it was being held aloft by the tree, as if it was trying to lift him to heaven manually. He looked back at Kinder who was now looking very sheepish, and turned back to pat the scarecrow on the shoulder.

Only then did the scarecrow open its eyes. A choked scream escaped from its stitched-up mouth. Francis jumped backwards, almost shitting himself in the process. He shouted at Kinder to grab the first aid kit from the car, but Kinder was rooted to the spot, mouth agog. The screaming stopped, the scarecrow's eyes rolled back in its head and closed. Kinder, coming to his senses, set off at a sprint. Francis wondered if the newbie was just going to jump in the front seat and leave him there. Instead, Kinder reappeared with the first aid kit in hand.

He took a deep breath and carefully touched the man again. No reaction this time. He tried to take the man's pulse but there was nothing. He really wished he'd put gloves on. Kinder pushed forward with the first aid kit but Francis waved him off. No amount of first aid was going to bring this poor bugger back to life. He told Kinder to call for an ambulance and a SOCO team and then wait in the car until they arrived. He stepped well back from the tree-man and pulled a pack of cigarettes from his pocket. He took out one for himself. It was upside-down. His lucky cigarette. He wasn't feeling lucky at all.

***

Francis was starting to feel the evening's chill, but he didn't move. He'd seen some shit before, but nothing like this. He dropped the butt of his cigarette and it joined the other three on the floor at his feet. He then lit a fifth without even thinking about it, his eyes never leaving the crime scene, if it even was a crime scene. He wasn't sure how long he had been stood there staring at the scarecrow man, he just knew it had been a while.

His thoughts drifted back to his Dad telling him stories about how the Vietcong used to torture captured American soldiers. They'd tie them to the floor face-down, above bamboo, and let it grow into and, ultimately, through them. This was basically what he was looking at on a grand scale. Somehow a birch tree had grown up and through the man in front of him, lifting him several feet in the air, its narrow trunk disappearing somewhere into his nether regions and dozens of small, and not so small, branches then forcing themselves out of him. It was almost as if the tree had provided the victim with a new timber skeleton. Two larger offshoots supported his arms, leaving him crucified without nails.

A black cat appeared out of nowhere and wrapped itself round his shins and ankles. Francis used the side of his foot to push it away from him and watched it slink off into the night. Filthy creatures, farm cats, he thought, always full of fleas, and he reached down and scratched an imaginary itch on his leg.

He stopped scratching at nothing, took a deep breath and stepped closer to the man. He could trace the tiny branches which had sewn the man's mouth shut by the silver sheen of their birch bark coating. Francis was surprised by how little blood there was anywhere, it was all very organic. Natural. He heard a vehicle pull up on the road behind him and looked back to see the ambulance had arrived. Out popped two over-eager paramedics who, once they saw what they were attending, had some debate who should act as the primary caregiver.

The unlucky loser stepped forward. It was a young chap Francis hadn't seen before, and he wondered if he ever would again after this. Francis gave him the nod and the paramedic approached the tree-man, touching his hand to his neck, looking for a pulse. Everyone remained silent. Francis knew the man was already dead, but it never hurt to check again. A mirror over the tree-man's only open airway and a second check for a pulse confirmed that the man was indeed dead. The paramedic turned back and gave a half shake of his head and shuffled off towards his colleague. Francis dropped his umpteenth cigarette onto the ground and screwed it into the earth with his heel. He looked over to Kinder.

'Get a portable shelter over him and wait for SOCO. Preserve everything'.'

He stood and looked once more at the poor soul intertwined with a tree. Just as he thought this day couldn't get any stranger, Francis noticed a shimmer on the ground at the dead man's feet. Something neither he, Kinder nor the paramedic had noticed earlier. Small daisy-like flowers had sprouted at the base of the trunk, in a line. As Francis got closer to them, he saw they had grown and arranged themselves as a word.

Nowell

***

The incident room was hardly a throng of activity, although they had made some small progress. The man had been identified as Steven Palmer, a local farmer with a decent amount of land, part of which he'd been found upon. What he'd been doing there before he was found was still a mystery. As it was still the night when he was discovered, the manpower assigned to the case was a skeleton crew consisting of whoever was around: in this case, Jenny Dennison, who just happened to be on duty tonight and was off brewing up, Chris Kinder and himself. Francis knew that this case was going to give him a headache, mainly because it was too bizarre for a rational explanation. Yet he knew that someone would have to come up with something plausible before the case could be officially closed, filed, swept under the rug and forgotten about. None of it sat well with Francis, so he hoped that his lightweight team could come up with something that might make a decent fist of it. The farmer deserved that at least.

***

Palmer had no next of kin to inform. That was a relief in some ways. The thing that was troubling Francis most at that moment were the flowers that had sprouted below the body.

'What is a Nowell? Has anyone Googled it?'

Kinder replied with frantic tapping on the keyboard in front of him and then looked up, clearly pleased that he'd found the answer.

'Well?'

'It's an ancient spelling of Noel. '

'Well that's no fucking use. Is it anything else?' Francis was too tired to pretend to be anything other than what he was. Annoyed. He had realised on the drive back to the station that he'd been caught up in the very thing he had tried to avoid. A full moon case.

'Failing that, it's just a surname.'

'Just a surname. Fuck me. Utterly unhelpful Kinder.'

Kinder ducked back down behind his screen and started tapping again, trying to find something of use that he could report. Jenny Dennison, who'd apparently crept into the room while Francis was laying into Kinder, placed a cup of tea at the side of Kinder's desk before walking over to Francis and giving him a stern look and a hot cup of coffee.

'Don't be a dick, Frank. He's trying.'

'Yeah, he fucking is,' Francis grumbled.

Nobody called him Frank, only Jenny, and he didn't like it much. He only let it slide with Jenny because he liked her. She was a good, modern copper. Intelligent, wise beyond her years and, despite her diminutive size, more than capable of kicking an arse or two if required. She'd be a real force to be reckoned with once she got out of uniforms and into CID. Assuming she didn't spend her days mollycoddling morons like Kinder.

'Frank, I was looking again at Palmer's next of kin. There's a Roger Nowell, deceased. Seems to be his great grandfather. Also listed at the same address. Died in 1972.'

'Well, that's something. Are they searching his house yet?'

'Underway now.'

'Okay, what about the type of flower then? What were they?'

Kinder sprang forth, seeing an opportunity to put himself back in Francis's good books. He confirmed that they were indeed daisies, were out of season and were not known for growing in the shape of words. Or spontaneously growing at night. Despite that information being unhelpful, he took Jenny's advice and decided to be less of a dick and leave it at that.

'Okay, good work.'

Kinder sat about six inches taller in his seat and grinned like an idiot. Francis shook his head ever so slightly and wondered how the newbie had even got through training.

✳✳✳

What he needed to do was think, and he always did his best thinking with a cigarette in his mouth. He'd been hoping that this was all some sort of practical joke using special effects, like on *The Walking Dead*, and that he and the others would appear on some video show where they pay people money for funny clips. Except this wasn't funny. It was horrific. He grabbed a new packet of cigarettes from the many packets that inhabited his top draw, both full and empty. He stuffed them in his coat pocket and left the room.

As he walked down the corridor, he knew at some stage he would have to notify the DCI about the case, who then would have to go on and notify the Chief Inspector. His issue with doing so was how he could describe it to anyone without them thinking he had gone off the deep end. No one would believe this story unless they'd seen it for themselves, and even then, he still wasn't sure if anyone would believe it. He still wasn't sure he did. It was vexing, alarming and disturbing all at once, but he still had a bit of time to figure it out. At some point the station would become much busier and it would be buzzing with what had happened, especially as it was only a small rural station in the Ribble Valley. Word would get around quickly and, once he passed this up the chain of command, the bigwigs from over in Preston would get involved. He and his motley crew would be pushed to the side and have no further role in the investigation. That, he thought, might not be such a bad thing.

***

Standing at the back gate to the police station, he opened his packet of cigarettes. He unwrapped them and pushed the foil and cellophane deep into his jacket pocket, where it crinkled with other accumulated rubbish. He took one out and put it in his mouth, then took out another, turned it tip down, and tapped it back into the packet. He closed the pack, lit the cigarette and looked about. It was nice and quiet. As much as he liked the station when it was full of hustle and bustle, he preferred it quiet even better. Even the great war between good and evil needed some respite, he mused. He watched a black cat saunter along the top of the surrounding fence, get to the end, turn around and do it again... as though it was pacing, or hunting. He could have sworn it was the cat he'd seen earlier at the tree-man scene, but black cats all looked the same. Still, seeing two in one night was odd, especially when he couldn't actually remember ever seeing one hereabouts before.

His musing was interrupted as the custody door unbolted and opened from the inside. He heard the murmuring of voices, then the heavy door was cast open and out stepped a diminutive woman. Very attractive, with dark curly hair, she immediately looked him right in the eyes and smiled. He braced himself for what was coming. It was his experience that women didn't usually smile at him at work. They often glowered at him, called him names, sometimes spat and occasionally resorted to violence. All that he took in his stride, but the smilers always put him on edge. There was something about a smile that he found to be as disarming as it was dangerous. Once, the girlfriend of a guy he had nicked for dealing had walked up to him, smiling all the way, explaining how grateful she was for his putting that monster behind bars. In a split-second, the smile was gone and she was trying to stab him with a kitchen knife that she'd pulled from nowhere. I'll take surliness over smiles any day, he thought. At least you know where you stand that way. Francis nodded to the near-sighted Duty Sergeant, who had just poked his head around the door like a mole poking his head above the ground. The Sergeant then slammed the custody door shut as if he'd smelled something he didn't like.

The woman introduced herself as Alice and asked him for a cigarette all in the same breath. Francis, not known for his generosity, especially to recently released prisoners, made an exception and offered her the packet.

'Oh, a lucky cigarette,' she remarked about the upside down one. 'Do you mind? I could use a bit of luck.'

He wasn't happy about her choice, but he nodded his approval, despite his annoyance. He liked his ritual, he liked saving the lucky cigarette until he felt he needed a bit of luck himself. She took it from the packet and rummaged in her pockets and then in her bum bag for a light. He hadn't thought anyone wore those things anymore. Still, it wasn't the strangest thing he'd seen tonight, not by a long shot. Francis took his own lighter out of his pocket and handed it to her, which she gratefully accepted.

'I haven't had one of these for twelve hours,' she said and

lit the cigarette. She took a deep draw on it and held it for good five seconds, before exhaling a thunderhead of a smoke. 'Better than sex, eh?'

Francis nearly choked on his own inhalation, which amused Alice no end.

'Sorry,' she grinned.

Francis sheepishly recovered his composure.

'So, are you just out as well?'

He took a deep breath and braced himself for everything that would happen next. Before he even said a word, she answered her own question.

'Oh, you work here, I get it. Not an easy job, I'm sure.' She took another drag of her cigarette.

'It has its moments,' was his reply.

'Oh, I'm sure it does.'

'So, you're just out, then?'

'Yes.'

Francis remained silent, letting the question hang in the air.

'I was arrested because my neighbour accused me of cursing her garden.'

'What, swearing at it?'

'No. Using black magic to stop things growing.'

'Oh. Do you get arrested for that often?'

'No, but yesterday she caught me standing in her garden drawing a pentagram with a five-litre bottle of bleach.'

Francis laughed out loud. 'Why would you do that?'

'Oh, I'm a particularly spiteful witch. It's all the rage nowadays.'

'Okay.' Francis dragged the word out a little longer than perhaps he should have. He changed the subject slightly. 'You've been released with a magistrate's date, right?'

'Yup. Providing I can behave myself until then. Friday, if you want to come.'

'I don't think me there will help your case one little bit.'

Alice considered his point and nodded her agreement.

Francis was enjoying this conversation no end. A little bit of levity with a lady who didn't want to assault or kill him was a wholly pleasant experience.

'No, you're right. Anyway, I've got to get going. Thanks for the smoke.'

'Yes, I'm supposed to be working, and you're welcome, Alice.'

'Nice meeting you, Francis,' she said as she walked away.

Once she was all but out of sight, Francis gave the quick entry knock to the custody suite, as he really couldn't be arsed with walking around the building again. It was only whilst waiting for the Duty Sergeant to answer the door that he realised that he hadn't given the woman his name. He never did, unless it was on police business, and never his first name. He turned to look for her, but there was no sign of her in the night. Sergeant Mole answered the door and Francis stepped back into the unpleasantly familiar smell of the strong cleaning product they used to clean everything down in custody. He asked Sergeant Mole about the woman he had just released.

'Ah, yes, she was an odd one. Gemma, hang on,' he ruffled some paperwork on his station and pulled out the right form. 'Gemma Clifton. Arrested for shoplifting. Not her first offense.'

'Not Alice?' he immediately countered, and then ventured, 'Are you sure that's the right paperwork you've got there?'

Desk Sergeant Mole gave Francis a withering look and looked back at the paperwork.

'No, definitely a Gemma,' he answered firmly.

Francis decided to chance his luck and asked if there was anything to do with bleach in the crime report. The Desk Sergeant sighed, rescanned the paperwork and pushed it into Francis's hands.

'Here, just look for yourself.'

Francis quickly skimmed through the report and it was exactly as the Sergeant had said. Shoplifting, held in the shop by the owner, a baseball bat. Attempting to take a four-pack of Bud and two cheap microwave curries. He smiled at that detail, as that could be his tea almost any night. He handed it back to the Sergeant, who only now seemed to begin to have questions forming. Francis waved his hands in the air and professed to having had a mad minute, then walked away as quickly as he could and headed back up to the incident room.

***

Francis returned to his colleagues, bemused, but actually in a better mood. He had somewhat enjoyed his conversation with the strange yet attractive woman he had met, despite the fact she was a criminal, had somehow known his name and seemed to be unsure of her identity. He assumed that at some stage in his career he'd had a run in with her or her family, and that was how she knew his name. The criminal pool was only so deep in and around the smaller towns surrounding Burnley, Clitheroe and Colne. He decided to put aside any idle fantasies he'd started to conjure because he knew that it was going nowhere, and that it was more than likely the next time he saw her she'd be in cuffs.

Kinder and Dennison were in animated discussion and pointing at whatever was on the computer screen, as he entered the room. They promptly stopped and looked at him uncomfortably. He stood waiting. Usually this would be when someone told him something of note, but they really seemed unwilling to venture anything. His good humour started to evaporate.

'Jesus fuck. Will one of you spit it out?'

'Well, firstly, they've searched Palmer's house,' said Dennison.

'And…'

'There's a note. Here.'

Dennison handed him a few photos that had obviously just been printed out. The first was a picture of a note on a table that read in neat handwriting, *She's coming for me*. Other than that, the rest of the photos showed a fairly ill-kept farmhouse with what seemed to be shelves of bottles of all shapes and sizes in every room.

'He thought someone was coming for him and he was a bottle collector?'

'According to Dave who was doing the search, they're witch bottles, originally designed to protect against magic. He saw some on *The Antiques Roadshow* a few weeks ago. Says they're worth a few quid as well'.

Francis put the pictures down on the desk. He didn't like where this was going at all. 'Okay so that isn't really what had you both so het up pointing at the screen though was it?'

'I just Googled Palmer and Pendle but with no notable results. Then I looked for Nowell and Pendle together, just to see if there was anything,' Dennison said.

'And?

Dennison was quiet. Kinder looked down at the floor. Francis took matters into his own hands and walked behind them both and leant over to look at the laptop screen. On the first page of Google, the top result was a Wikipedia entry, *The Pendle Witches*. In the paragraph accompanying the headline was the name Roger Nowell.

'Right. And? You're both not telling me that you think a witch flew back from the what the eighteenth century?'

'Seventeenth, sir,' Kinder chirped.

Francis just glowered. 'And this witchy-poo planted a tree in that poor bastard. And he knew she was coming and he let her do it anyway.' Francis's voice got louder and louder. 'Is that what you are telling me?'

The room again fell silent. Francis pulled his coat off from over his chair and put it on. He was sure Dennison and Kinder felt his anger warming the room. He took a deep breath and tried to regain his composure. This whole situation was bad enough without these two putting it down to witchcraft.

He tried again, but this time more with a more measured tone. 'Well? Is that what you're telling me? Two professional law enforcement officers are telling me it's witchcraft?'

He watched the two of them squirm beneath his question. He almost expected it from Kinder. But he was astounded that Dennison would even consider it. So much so, he wondered if his estimation of her abilities to make something of herself in the job were misplaced.

"Fuck this, I've had enough. Fucking witchcraft. Ring Burnley and get a hold of Lawes or Morris or whoever is supposed to be on duty tonight. Let them deal with this shitshow.'

***

With that rant he left the room, slamming the door behind him. He was pissed off at the pair of them, especially Dennison, for going down such a stupid path. Crime was committed by criminals, not witches. No matter how bizarre a crime might at first seem, both the rational explanation and the criminal motive behind it always became apparent, as long as you looked in the right place. And looking in the right place was something Francis knew he had a knack for. What he was really struggling with at the moment, though, was the "how".

The notion that poor tree-man Palmer had been tied to a tree sapling for the last fifteen years or so without anyone noticing was clearly nonsense. Then there was the note. The bottles were a red herring, he was sure. Some strange collection Palmer had. So there had to be something else. There had to be something he was missing, maybe some new chemical that caused excessive growth in plants. He made a mental note to get Dennison to chase that idea down tomorrow.

He'd been that lost in his own thoughts, he realised he had wandered through the station and out into the car park to his car. He decided he was having a beer tonight, and that curry he was craving. He checked his watch and figured he'd be just about be in time for an order before they shut, so he gave them a call and ordered Beef Madras with pilau rice and a few poppadoms. The man on the end of the phone recognised him by voice and said he'd have his order with him in about twenty-five minutes. That gave Francis just enough time to get home and be ready for it.

***

Francis walked into the kitchen, took a clean plate out of the cupboard, gave it a quick polish with a tea towel and set it down on the worktop. He then got out a fork and a spoon and placed them on the plate, ready for when his meal came. From the fridge he took out one of a dozen or so bottles of lager and flipped the top with his wall mounted Motorhead bottle opener. He looked at his watch and considered breaking out the Hoover, then decided it was way too early in the morning for that. For a single man, it was remarked on by the few who ever entered his house, he kept the place very clean and tidy. He liked order. He liked things to be straightforward. Yet the events of the night were frustratingly anything but straightforward. He struggled to think of a possible way a tree could grow through a person in a farmer's field in Worston. He checked his watch and wondered where his food was. While he was waiting, he sat in his chair and put Netflix on, selected *keep watching* and clicked on a documentary about tigers. He took a big swig of his beer, sat back in his comfy chair and started the process of trying to erase the troubles of the night just gone from his mind.

***

He woke with a jolt and checked his watch. It was after 2am. He also noted that he was wearing handcuffs, and he was tied to a chair. It wasn't the chair he had sat in, but one of the chairs at his dining table. On the table in front of him was his meal, set out for two, complete with a side plate of poppadoms, mango chutney for dipping them in, and two glasses of water. Alice was sat across from him, heartily tucking into what seemed to be his curry.

'The Raj is the best, isn't it?'

He sat in stunned silence, trying to understand exactly what was going on, questions flooding his mind. What? Where? Why and how? When he finally decided which one to ask first, Alice stopped him before he even opened his mouth.

'Don't panic. I'll explain, but eat your food before it gets cold.'

As much as Francis really loved a curry, he really didn't want to eat anything anymore. Despite his lack of appetite, he took a couple of clumsy forkfuls with his cuffed hands to buy himself a bit of time. The hot richness of the spices which he usually so enjoyed caught at the back of his throat and made him cough. Alice looked up with concern on her face, which then turned to mirth.

'Too hot for you?' She flicked her hair a little, laughed and went back to eating her food.

Francis shook his head and carefully reached for the glass of water which was next to his plate. It wasn't easy trying to drink with handcuffs on, and some dribbled down his chin.

'So, Alice, Gemma? What do I call you?'

'Alice. Gemma is just one of many aliases.'

'Why do you have aliases?'

'Is that the question you really want to ask?'

'No. Why am I tied up?'

'So we can have a meal together.'

'Why?'

'The meal was a nicety on my part, to be honest. I thought you'd enjoy it.'

'What happens now, then?'

'We finish our meal. I don't know about you, but I'm starving.' Alice broke off a piece of poppadum and dipped it in the mango chutney before she went back her main plate.

Francis thought his day had ended poorly before he fell asleep. Now, he was wondering if he hadn't woken up in the very worst of nightmares. He really didn't know how to broach the subject of why she was there. Fortunately, he didn't have to. Again, Alice seemed to know his question before he did.

'You are Francis John Whittle, son of John Whittle, son of Francis Whittle and so on and so on, all the way back to 1612. Now, the 1612 Whittle, he was a real bastard. He's the reason I'm here.'

Francis was perplexed. That was the second time 1612 had come up tonight. This had to be some sort of elaborate joke that everyone was involved in. Alice, Kinder, Dennison, Desk

Sergeant Mole, all of them. This was way too unusual for a man like him. He certainly did not like having the power he was so used to being taken away from him. He was beginning to understand how the people he arrested felt, handcuffed to a table and being interrogated. Except he was the one still asking the questions. He just wasn't getting answers that made sense.

'The original Francis Whittle killed some of my friends, for witchcraft.'

'I really don't understand.'

'Let me put it in terms you do. Earlier today, I killed the last Nowell. The Nowell of 1612 was The High Sheriff of Lancashire, one of the men responsible for the Witch Trials. I lured him into his field and killed him. Shortly, I'll kill you too.'

'I had nothing to do with any of that nonsense.'

As soon the words came out of his mouth, he knew his error, but it was too late. Alice left her chair and launched herself across the table. She stunned him with an almighty slap across the face. She then recovered herself and sat back down opposite.

'Yes, you do.'

Her volatility made him very, very nervous. It meant she was as unpredictable as she was dangerous.

'The Whittle of 1612 was a torturer for the Crown.'

'But I'm not.'

'Your name is written in blood. I'm going to erase it.'

'I think you might need some help, Alice. Can I get you some help?' Francis hoped he wasn't overdoing the sincerity, but if he could keep things amiable, maybe he could get out of this situation with nothing but bruised pride and a story he'd never tell.

'I know it's hard to understand. Let me make you a believer.'

She raised her hands in the air and, as she did, up went the plates they had both been eating from. She swirled her hands and the plates span around the room, although their contents, remarkably, stayed in place.

'There were over three hundred people present or involved with the trials,' Alice said as she waved her hands, dancing the plates around the room. 'Two hundred and twenty-seven, different bloodlines. I've expunged fifty-two of them over the years. Ended them completely. You will make fifty-three.'

She placed the plates back down in front of them gently and flashed Francis a knowing smile. He thought that smile suggested that maybe he hadn't seen anything yet.

'If you're not hungry, perhaps you'd like a cigarette?'

She pulled what looked like his packet from her pocket, took one out, lit it and then flipped it into the air. She caught it using the same trick she'd used with the plates and guided it over to Francis's lips. He leant forward and gratefully accepted it, took a deep drag and considered his options. He could shout, but his neighbours probably wouldn't wake up in time to do anything significant. He thought he could overpower her if he moved quickly; he doubted flying plates or any other parlour tricks could stop him from doing that. He took another long draw on his cigarette and exhaled. He spat the cigarette away, shoved the table hard into Alice, who was immediately knocked to the floor. He leapt up still in his seat and smashed himself backwards against the wall to break it. Pieces of pine fell away and he shrugged the washing line he was bound with over his head, leaving just his hands cuffed. Alice was still on the floor. He headed through the lounge to the front door. He reeled as something hit him on the back of the head. As he turned to confront his assailant, one of the dinner plates from the table slapped him in the face and then clattered to the floor. He turned back to the door and tried to open it, but it was stuck fast. As he turned around to see where Alice was, a glass hit him first in the face, then again in the side of the head, which made the room spin. It hit him once more and everything went black.

***

The moon, full and red, was the only thing Francis could see laid on his back. He rolled onto his side and found himself looking straight into the green eyes of a cat. He jerked his head back and the cat hissed and waved a front paw at him, like it was going to give him a good boxing. It changed its mind and ran off into the night.

He looked around and recognised Pendle Hill immediately. Though now it looked different. The reddish-pink hue of the moon had turned the banks of the hill a deep blood-red. He was at a reservoir, one of the small ones, maybe Ogden or Black Moss. It was hard to tell from where he lay. He was also fairly sure he was naked, given the creeping wet chill he felt everywhere his body touched the ground. Alice came from out of the darkness and loomed over him. There was no trace of the nice Alice he'd met outside of custody.

'I'll make this easy, Francis. Confess!'

'To what? Untie me. This has gone far enough.'

'No, Francis. It hasn't even started. If you confess to being of witch-killer blood, I'll make it easy on you.'

'You're fucking crazy.'

'Right, we'll get to it then. Your ancestor seemed to enjoy this one.'

Alice began muttering an incantation and the bushes behind her started rustling. The sound became louder and louder until a collective snap cracked the air. Francis craned his neck to see what was going on, but he didn't have to wait long to find out. A single hawthorn spike hovered before his nose. Focusing past it, Francis could see the air was tumbling with them, thousands and thousands of the wooden thorns, all playing joyfully in the air, like a swarm of bees. He twisted his head to one side, having an idea of what might be coming. The spike that was loitering with intent in front of his face followed.

'Let's start slowly.'

The spike suddenly jabbed Francis in the left eye, in and out. As quickly as the pain was there, it was gone. He felt a trickle of what he assumed to be blood, or whatever was inside of his eyeball, trickle down the side of his face.

'This was a favourite back in the day. They even had people who specialised in it. Prickers, they were called. Trust me, though, I'm better than them.'

With that, Alice launched the first wave of thorns at Francis. White-hot pain seared him. Through closed eyes he could see a kaleidoscope of colours and lines. Then it was gone. He panted his relief, but it was only temporary. The spikes came again. Then again. Then again. He screamed through his closed mouth: he didn't dare open it for fear of the torturous pins getting inside. Just as he felt he could take no more, the thorns stopped.

'Are you ready to confess?'

Francis shook his head through sheer stubbornness. The truth was he wasn't sure how much longer he could endure.

'That's okay. You will.'

The flying needles came again. They pierced every part of him. He rolled over in an attempt to shield parts of himself, but all he did was give them a fresh canvas. He couldn't take any more. He opened his mouth and started screaming.

'I confess! I confess! Ahhh. I confess!'

The thorns continued their work. In and out, in and out. Only when his screams became incoherent did she accept his confession. The needles withdrew from his tortured body and buzzed about in the air. Alice grabbed him and dragged him with unnatural strength backwards, sitting him up against a tree.

'Good. I accept your guilt.'

The hawthorn points all fell to the floor and she sat next to him. She pulled his head into her lap and stroked his hair, almost lovingly. She stopped long enough to light another cigarette and place it in Francis's mouth. He coughed violently and spat it out.

As he lay there fighting for breath, he tried to shake her off him, but her grip remained firm. He could smell the cigarette burning and assumed Alice was smoking it instead. He tried to look around. The kaleidoscope effect had worn off as soon as the needles had stopped. For reasons he couldn't comprehend, one eye was untouched while the other was ruined. He struggled to focus. He could see shades of light and dark, and a great pink blob, which he knew was the moon. He felt Alice moving to stand up: she gently lifted him into his previous seated position, placing his head back against the rough surface of the tree. He had a sudden floating sensation. His immediate thought was Alice was moving him again. She did seem unusually strong. He took a deep breath and tried to force himself to breathe through it. He thought it was maybe an adrenaline comedown from what he'd been through, but quickly realised his initial instinct had been right: he was being levitated.

She smiled at him.

'I want you to know that I liked you,' she said. With a casual gesture of her hand, she raised the thorns once more. Then she waved them forward and, this time, they came thicker, faster and harder. He was engulfed by them, but they didn't fly in and out. They burrowed into him, each one going in to the hilt. As he screamed, they flew into his mouth, both eyes, even into his genitals and rectum. Every inch of his flesh was impaled. Even then, he wasn't dead, nor was Alice finished with him. She raised both arms in the air, lifting Francis until he was a good six or seven metres up. She manoeuvred him over to the reservoir and then smashed him downwards.

He almost bounced off the water, so great was the impact. His chest was crushed and he felt several ribs give way. He drew in a single ragged gasp for air, before the invisible hand dragged him under the water. He held his breath as long as he could, resisting the urge to inhale. He wasn't sure how long he was held there before he felt himself rising again. He burst out of the water, sobbing for air. Without warning, he was pulled down once more. Panic grew as he realised he was being ducked, like the witches of old, like Alice's friends had been. He knew none survived this torture. If she held him under, he would drown. If he floated, it was proof of guilt, and execution would follow.

His lungs were about to burst. A part of him wanted to succumb to it, to end the ordeal. The icy waters of the reservoir would be the last he knew of this world. As he was about to give in, he was rushed back up to the surface.

'Looks like you're a floater, Francis. One final try.'

She slammed him beneath the water a third time. The hidden hand that held him gripped him tighter, squeezing his broken ribs, forcing him to exhale the little air he had in his lungs. He was dragged right down to the very bottom, the pressure pushing in on his eardrums causing him to feel light-headed.

His life flashed before him, up to the night just gone, to today, to being here at the bottom of a reservoir. He hadn't believed in witches or magic, or even known about his ancestry of witch-finders. That was what had caused his downfall. He believed now, but it was too late. There was no more panic, only acceptance. He hoped Dennison and Kinder somehow found it between them to discover what had happened to him. He hoped they avenged him by catching Alice, but he couldn't see how they could beat her in a fair fight. Still, they believed, and they'd have a few years to try and figure it out. If only there was some way he could help. He sat scratching at his thigh... until he lost consciousness. He jolted awake as water filled his lungs. He had taken a spasmodic breath. Although his mouth was open, his windpipe had closed, preventing any more water from filling his chest. It hurt more than anything he'd been through that night. This was a different type of hurt. It hurt so much he couldn't even writhe. He knew he was dead now. His body was just going through the final motions of trying to survive because it didn't know any better. He willed it to stop fighting. The battle was lost. Within a few moments, he had surrendered eternally.

***

Once she was certain Francis was dead, Alice moved some rocks around underneath the water to hold him down. She didn't want him to be found anytime soon, if at all. With Francis firmly secured beneath the dark water, she realised how tired she was. Two killings in a night had taken their toll. The amount of magic she had consumed during this cycle astounded her. She was certainly continuing to get stronger. When she'd started out on this path of vengeance, she'd had to resort to poisonings and stabbings. Yet the more she'd practised her Dark Art, the more she'd unleashed her unholy powers on others, the more she'd become adept at wielding them. Each time, however, there was a cost. The use of so much energy withered her. Her skin felt thin, her vision was less acute and arthritic pain wracked her body. She needed to bathe in the cool silver light of the moon. The pink Witch's Moon enabled her to release power; the silver moon was to draw it in, allowing her to restore body and spirit.

Right now, she was beyond exhausted. She had burned through every last bit of energy that she had stored since the previous Witch's Moon. She sat down heavily under the tree where she had sat holding Francis. The black cat climbed up next to her, curled himself into the tiniest ball and started to purr. They were both content with their night's work. She looked up at the bright, blood moon. She felt weak, wrinkled and used up. By this time tomorrow, she would be just another little old lady going about her business, waiting for death. Except it was never her that Death came for. There were many others in line ahead of her. She thought, all things considered, that the last of the Whittles had died well. He'd been brave and resolute right to the end. Even though she didn't forgive him his family's sins, she respected his ending.

She produced her pocketbook from the highly unfashionable bum bag she was wearing, opened the page and crossed out Francis Whittle's name. She then flicked through to a different page. Her finger ticked off each date as she remembered who she had killed and how. This was her personal crusade. It was her duty to collect the souls of the relatives of those who had almost caught her back in 1612. She hadn't survived the trials just to disappear into obscurity. By the time she was finished, and let the world know what she'd achieved, she'd be a legend. She spared a second to remember her fallen sisters, who had been taken from this world by torture, starvation, beatings, rape, drowning and more. The degradations were as numerous as the delightful new ways she came up with for killing the kin of those who had wronged her kind. Killing the last of a bloodline was always so satisfying, especially this one.

She wasn't sure she was done with the police officers of

Pendle just yet, but she knew she needed to be patient. She must wait until the next Witch's Moon, time she would use first to recover and then to conduct further research into bloodlines of those who had brutalised her kin. There were so many still to find, but one day all those who had ever thought to persecute witches would be undone.

As she got up to walk away, she looked over at where Francis Whittle's submerged body was. Bubbles fizzed to the surface and, when she stood up on her tip toes, she could see they formed letters, letters that spelled a single word.

Whittle

Wytch *f* ynder

By Michael Conroy

I

Clouds converged on the hilltop as the breeze ran its fingers
through the dew-spattered grass. Matthew Procter watched
from afar as the villagers trod their way up the slope. He saw no
storm on the horizon, and yet, as though expecting lightning,
all the hairs on the back of his neck prickled.

He laid his hand over his pocket and patted his coin purse.
Clink-clink. The village appeared barren from such distance,
as many outland settlements did to civilised folk. The wooden
houses and little church, mere specks, looked like minor details
in a mediocre painting.

Stepping back from the edge of the hill, he drew his cloak
around him, when a gust of wind blew off his black capotain.
Bending down to retrieve it, the fluttering of wings caught his
ear. On the outstretched bough of an oak tree perched a Crow.

The Bird, uttering no sound, gazed at him as he donned
his hat. Behind its small black eyes, there seemed an uncanny
intelligence, and curious interest in the forthcoming spectacle.
It stared and stared at him as the wind muttered. He had seen a
bird just like it the day John Procter, his Father, had died.

Smithy Jenson's brown helmet of hair bobbed up over the
edge of the hilltop. The Youth wore his doublet fastened to

the neck and his boots had been muddied by the climb. No cloak hung on his shoulders, so the Boy hugged himself for warmth. "Goode morrow, Matthew, what cheere?"

"There be no cheere in these darke times, Smithy."

Patches of stubble covered Smithy's pale pockmarked face. "Too righte. They be heading this waye now."

He heard the jeering villagers tramping up the hill. And the Woman, too, screaming as though anyone would listen: "My children! Let me see my children!"

The Priest wore a purple stole over his shoulders. "And, thou Son of Man, thus saith the Lorde God; speake unto every feathered fowle, and to every beaste of the fielde, assemble Yourselves, and come; gather Yourselves on every syde to my Sacrifyce…"

The Woman dragged her feet like a farmyard animal, hair dishevelled, shift soiled, as Blacksmyth and Son, John and James Chambers, escorted her by the arms. "Please, don't do this! Oh God, please!"

A noose dangled from a branch above head height. Two dozen villagers of all professions gathered on the hilltop, tossing stones. She whimpered as the village wives, her former friends, called her "Whore," "Jezebel," and "Wytch."

"Damn you, damn you all—" A pebble split her forehead, knocking the breath out of her. The Blacksmyth bound her hands and stood her atop a wooden barrel. Noose tight around her neck, she struggled, on her toes, to keep the barrel steady. Rocking back and forth on the slanting ground, she took on the appearance of someone drowning – desperate to remain afloat.

"Annabelle Chambers," Matthew said. "I shall give you one last chance before God to admit your crimes. Our Lorde can be merciful, but only to those willing to repent… You stande accused of being a Wytch… How do you pleade?"

She spat at him. "Not guiltie!"

The crowd jeered. He wiped his doublet with his glove. "Do you heare, friends? Not guiltie, she sayes… Tell me, who here is without Sin?"

"Helpe me, James," she cried. "Please, don't let them do this."

The Blacksmyth's Son did not meet her eye. "If you love me," she said, "you won't do this…"

"Don't tempte Him!" spat the Blacksmyth, corners of his moustache twisting into a snarl. "You'll bring no more harm to our family, nor no one else's, Wytch."

"But she's my wife," said the Son. "How can we let this happen? It isn't right."

Matthew pointed. "Have sense, Boye! She castes heapes of Trouble on those that cross her. Did she not disappear your own new-born Babe – to satiate her Master's Coven?"

"No, no," she cried. "I would never!"

He removed his hat and placed it over his heart. "The childe had not yet seen baptisme… Now he, too, will be damned… Goode People, let us heare your accusations, and put all talke of innocence to bedde."

Angela Johnson, mother, sobbed as she spoke. "She strangles babies in the wombe…"

Garrick Hardwood, senile veteran of the Nine Years' War, raised his stick and said, "She talkes to Spirits in animal skinne and castes *spelles* upon her enemies!"

Nicholas Benton, apprentice Bootmaker cupped his hands and shouted, "She crawles into your bedde at nighte and puts uncleane thoughts in your heade!"

Hardwood piped up again, "She's put thoughts in my heade!"

Georgina Baker, Innkeeper's Wife, counted on her fingers: "Her breade stayes softe for dayes… She ruines croppes…

Her eyes are greene… Her haire is curlie like the Devil's…"

Agatha Mayhew, unmarried School Mistress, raised her voice. "I have it on goode accounte she enjoys fornicating with livestocke."

William Baker, Innkeeper, was quick to add, "I've seen her dancing naked in the woodes, I have!"

"Only in your dreames, Husband," said Mrs Baker, scowling first at him, and then at the accused.

Margaret Poultice, the Milkmaid's Daughter, a fair-haired girl humbled by God with a large, erect mole on her left cheek, was last to testify. "Her clothes are alwayes cleane… and her breath is tolerable."

Matthew replaced his hat, then raised his hand. "Now, a demonstration…" Here the Crow fluttered its wings and cawed six times in succession. The Blacksmyth shooed the Bird, but it would not be put off.

"Let it remaine," Matthew said. "We have seen many Omens these days past, what's one more?"

Taking the fat end of a needle, and brushing the Woman's shift to one side, he pricked the birthmark on her shoulder. "Do you see now? I have pricked her with this needle, and yet she does not bleede!"

The crowd gasped, for it was as he'd said, not a drop of blood.

"The marke of the Beaste is upon her, make no mistake, for t'is how he knows his servants. And did you not see her floate in yonder river? T'was not God saved her from drowning, but the Devil, for he wishes her to live on and do more Wickedness."

The Woman shrieked. "Lies, you conspire against me."

Matthew shook his head. "Annabelle Chambers, for crimes of Wytchcraft, Heresy, Diabolism, and Infanticide, you will hang by the necke until you are deade."

Whether she was smiling or sneering, he could not tell, for

blood had stained her teeth. He looked away as she screamed to the village folk, "Damn you all… You'll be deade soone too—"

THUMP—CRACK!

The villagers fell silent – and even the wind gave way to the creaking of the rope. Looking off over the moors, Matthew caught a glimpse of her red hair from the corner of his eye, then made his way through the crowd.

Smithy shouted after him, but he ignored the Boy. The creaking of the rope still reached his ear – he heard nought else as he descended the hill. Nought but the sound of his coin purse clinking against his breast.

II

Firelight flickered on the walls, flashing across watchful eyes. Hops and pipe smoke in the air. Matthew sat alone, as the rain pattered against the windowpanes. A draught whistled under the door to the inn.

The Innkeeper set a tankard of foamy ale down on the table. Mathew passed him a coin. Lingering, the Proprietor asked, "How much longer do you think you'll be staying then, Mr Wytchfynder? Now that the matter has been settled?"

Matthew eyed him. "I shall not remaine long. Leave me be if you would."

The Innkeeper frowned and retreated to his spot by the kegs. His wife emerged from a dark passage behind the barrels. A coif covered her head and she wore a flour-marked apron over her petticoat. Their daughter wore a burgundy dress with the top two buttons unfastened, braided brown hair dangling over her breast.

Matthew sipped ale as the fire crackled. Around the inn, folk sat in silence, drinking by candlelight. He peeled back his sleeve to reveal a dry red rash. Like the Devil's anus, it itched.

The door clattered open, wind shrieking until it closed again. "A flagon of ale, goode innkeeper!"

Matthew rolled his eyes. "Smithy, there is haye in your haire… And you smelle of fornication."

Smithy sat down and grinned. "I'm a growing Boye," he said, parting his wet bob with his fingers. "I had no choice but to seeke shelter in the barne, Matthew. T'was only then I made the Lady's acquaintance."

Matthew shook his head. "You followed her in there, I suspect."

"A roll in the haye is to be expected in such weather."

"Your Mother would be proude."

"Oh, she was gladde to be rid – would've solde me off to paye the Piper hadn't you come along to rescue me. *'You're a layabout and a pervert,'* she saide. All I did was kisse my cousin!"

Matthew sighed. "Let us quit this place on the morrow." Sipping ale, he couldn't help but linger on the Innkeeper's Daughter. "Our efforts will be needed elsewhere."

Indeed, they had dallied too long. The people were poor. They could not afford another Wytch. How he longed for escape – for civilisation, convenience, bustling city streets. Anything but these quiet moors. He'd been doing this job all his life, it seemed, and now the silence surrounded him on all sides. He struggled to keep his own thoughts in check.

Judas… Fraud… Murderer… How could anyone live the waye he did…?

The Innkeeper's Daughter set a tankard of ale down for Smithy. She smelled like apples and fresh-baked bread. Matthew scratched his arm, conjuring in his imagination her naked chest, then gave her a second look. Her brown eyes, speckled with green, held his gaze.

"Something to saye, Girl?"

Her parents muttered to one another, glancing over at Matthew's table as they cleaned cups and tankards. "I feare only you can helpe us, Mr Wytchfynder."

Smithy raised his tankard, drank, and wrapped an arm around her waist. "This here's a Man of God, Girl. He's no goode to you. I, on-the-other-hand, am up to the task—*Ouch!*" Smithy pulled a face, ale sloshing onto his lap, as she twisted his ear.

"There'll be none of that," she said, frowning like a Puritan. "I'm soone to be married."

Matthew swallowed. "What a lucky younge groome." For her bodice, cut into a delicate V-shape, did little to hide the ripeness of her youth. How old was she? Old enough to marry. Old enough for... so many things.

The firelight flickered in her eyes. "Mr Wytchfynder," she whispered, cheeks flushed pink. "There's something in the woodes."

He mustered a smile. "Badgers, foxes, owls..."

She frowned. "You don't understande. The woodes – they swallowe children up. They go in... and don't come backe oute."

"Wolves have beene known to snatch helplesse new-bornes when their Mothers aren't looking."

"Wolves," she scoffed. "The leaste of our problemmes are wolves. Annabelle Chambers was not without Sin, but it need not have beene her up on the hill. That's all I'll saye... Whatever tooke that babie of hers is still at worke. T'is in the aire, the raine, the trees, can't you feele it?"

He hadn't felt much of anything in a long time.

"We're all sinners. Even you, Matthew Procter."

"How dare—"

She warned him with her finger. "One Evil does not banish another. Hanging an innocent Woman," and here she placed a hand upon her belly, "will not save our children. Evil lives in those woodes. You must roote it oute."

He brought his face close to hers. "I don't believe in Evil. And I have not the patience for these childishe fancies. *Wytchcraft* is not... a common affliction. You'll find most superstitions originate from... long-forgotten, unfortunate accidents. There is nothing else to saye."

She shook her head, brow wrinkling, reached into her bosom, and dropped a small bag of gold onto the table.

A pittance. Wouldn't buy a decent paire of bootes, let alone a whore. He caught her gaze. Then again, perhaps the bride-to-be might be persuaded to up the ante. *If she knows what's goode for her.* "Into the woodes, you saye? Like Chambers' babie?"

She nodded. "You should ask Father Nicholas."

He and Smithy looked at each other. "And what would he know about it?"

The Girl glanced left and right. "There are rumours about him."

"Rumours?"

She shook her head. "I can't saye anymore. I've paide you goode money, now give me your worde."

He watched Smithy jiggle the contents of the velvet bag. "What's your name?" he asked her.

"Belinda, Sir."

"I would not have my dayes idly wasted, Belinda. Time is precious. And there's only so much satisfaction in gold."

His arm prickled as she leaned in closer, and said, under her breath, so that only he could hear, *"Don't worrie, I'll make it worth your while,"* and before the words had registered, she'd withdrawn into the gloom of the inn. He watched as she whispered sweet nothings to some shadowy patron whose face he couldn't see. A hand on her hand. A kiss on the cheek. Firelight in her eyes.

***

III

The morning sky was tarnished grey. Darker than days past. Tall silver birches backed the church grounds. A small, crumbling graveyard lay before them, its tombstones arranged around a dead oak tree, as though all their owners' misfortunes had originated beneath it. The modest stone walls housed stained-glass windows that shone dimly in the daylight. *Christ in Gethsemane, Lazarus, The Golden Calf.* Too Catholic-looking, Matthew thought. His hand tingled as they drew close.

A Crow clung to the weathervane atop the modest steeple – peering with its beady eye. "Mangie thing," Smithy said. "Shall I throwe my Boote at it, Matthew?"

The Bird watched without making a sound. "T'is just a Bird, Smithy."

Inside the church, wooden reliefs adorned the walls, and empty pews sat crooked and dusty. Sloth was the Devil's daily bread, and to scorn one's Parents a Sin – his Father had warned him of that.

Smithy whistled. "Smells a bit off in here, dunnit?"

"Some variety of incense, I suspect."

"Like a dog's jism, it smells, Matthew."

At the end of the aisle lay a simple altar draped in cloth. Candle sticks and a jewel-encrusted gold goblet stood atop the soiled white sheet. A hefty bible of King James sat open on display – upside down. He turned it right way up. *Fear came upon every Soul: and many Wonders and Signs…* A large dark stain marked the sheet covering the altar – like spilled wine.

Footsteps and creaking floorboards. "Damn you, childe, wave that thing over this way or I'll beate you with it!"

Father Nicholas emerged from a curtained passage behind the altar, shoving forward a fair-haired young altar boy. The Father, barefoot, wore lavish purple robes. He crossed himself and blessed the air sporadically as he shuffled along. The Boy, no more than twelve, swung a golden incense burner. He spotted Matthew and the burner clattered against the floor, sound echoing off the walls.

The Priest's eyes flickered with rage. "You little Sinner, watch what you're doing!" Here the Father grabbed the Boy and dropped him over his knee. He then smacked the Boy's backside with the palm of his hand. "You're hurting me!" the Boy yelped, but the Father didn't stop – just kept smacking him over and over until red in the face and the Boy in tears.

Matthew stared, hands hovering by his sides, not knowing what to say. "Father, stoppe…"

But Father Nicholas didn't hear him – a twisted grin had spread across the Priest's lips, and he was almost salivating, every breath hoarse and ragged, as he beat the helpless Boy.

"Father, stoppe," he said again, and Father Nicholas shot him a look like a hungry Lion. His wild eyes betrayed his excitement.

Matthew squirmed, for he felt each strike upon himself, as he remembered his own boyhood beatings. Stomach queasy, he trembled as he shouted, "Father, stoppe hitting me!" Then he half-gasped, realising what he'd said. His Father's voice echoed in his head – *What're you doing wi' that? Put it down, Boye, or I shall take off my belte…*

The Priest's hand hovered over the sobbing Boy's backside. Father Nicholas smiled. Gently rubbing the Child's shoulder, he grabbed him by the collar, and planted a kiss on his forehead. "I don't know what came over me," the Priest said, smiling, as he pushed the Boy to one side.

The Father, still down on one knee, welcomed Matthew and Smithy with his arms outstretched. "I'm so gladde you've come. Both of you." The smell of incense grew more pungent now as it filled the room. Sage or wormwood. Or something more bitter, like wolfsbane.

Matthew steadied himself. "What afflicts you, Father?"

The Priest rose to his feet on flabby, hairy legs. Matthew glimpsed a fleeting flash of pudgy genitals as the Father rearranged his robes. "I am filled with such Joye," he said, and anointed the air before him with an invisible sword.

Matthew sneered. "T'is ungodly."

"Christ is all things to all Men, my Son. Does your arm trouble you?"

Matthew began to seethe. "No distractions shall keepe me from my worke. Those who deale Evilly will meete the Noose. I always finde them oute."

The Priest shrugged his shoulders. "Yes, well, go finde them oute somewhere else. Your worke here is complete... I wouldn't linger too long if I were you." The Father then bowed, kicked the incense burner, and ushered the altar Boy back behind the curtain out of sight.

Smithy chuckled. "I suppose we'll have to reimburse younge Belinda."

Matthew raised his hand and made a fist. "Let's not get ahead of ourselves, Smithy. We must follow the traile wherever it leades."

"Because God is with us all the way," Smithy said.

If there is a God... In the church grounds, a sudden wind scattered the brown leaves. He heard the weathervane creak as it spun atop the steeple – the Crow had flown he knew not where. Though the day had hardly progressed, he felt, inexplicably, that it would be dark soon. The trees loomed ahead. They were so close together, you could see nothing within. It didn't matter. T'was as Smithy had said. God was with them.

***

Slipping through the trees, they kept to the narrow path, daring not to step off it, lest they lose their way. Every turn took them deeper and deeper into the woods. In such close quarters, they'd be made short work of by Bandits or Royalists, although Smithy claimed to carry a dagger on his person.

"Are we not there yet, Matthew?" The Boy's chatter seemed never-ending. "My bootes are rubbing, and I've got a banging headache. T'is hard to breathe in these woodes."

A thick, warm smell hung in the air, somewhat sweet, somewhat sickly, like rotten fruit – fermented apples. "I feel eyes upon us," Smithy said. "And my mouthe's drier than Cromwell's bunions."

"Have courage. This too will passe." To hear Smithy crunching through the leaves behind him was a great comfort, for he caught no other sound. No birds. No insect scuttling. But for the noise of their passing, all was an unnatural silence.

The rash had spread beyond his wrist. It prickled up his arm. *Better not to think about it.* He'd said the same at Pendle. *We're all sinners… Even you, Matthew Procter.*

Arriving at an empty crossroads, he brushed cobwebs from his face. He felt things creeping through his hair and under his clothes. The atmosphere weighed upon them, their every breath an effort. And the trees, all uniform in the dim light, crowded in behind them.

The route to the left was snared by brambles. The path ahead was an impossible tangle of tree limbs and spider webs. They went right, although the way was increasingly overgrown and obscured by leaf litter.

"Tell us a storie of your adventures, Matthew?"

"I would rather not, Smithy."

"Oh go on. Tell us the one where you went to Germany."

"I've tolde you that storie before. I would not dwell on it here."

"Do it for Smithy. Anything to keepe my thoughts from straying."

The Boy was right. Perhaps a historie might lighten their spirits. Then again, the stories he had to telle all ended the same waye.

"My birth parents died when I was younge. For much of my life, I was raised by my guardian, Jeremiah Hopkins. There was money to be made hanging Wytches in those days. Worde had reached him from the continente of an outlandish set of trials going on in Germany. It didn't take us long to track down the source of the rumours – a town called Würzberg.

"But by the time we arrived, the Burnings had already begun... I saw a Girl of thirteen sentenced for conspiring with her Neighbour's Cat. The way she screamed as her haire caught fire – it sounded almost like laughter—" Smithy dug his fingers into Matthew's shoulder. "Ow! Blast you, Boye, what ailes you?"

No one stood in his shadow, and, worse still, the path ahead had vanished. Twigs snapped underfoot. "Smithy?" he whispered, as leaves rustled behind him. Heart thumping in his chest, his feet took off with him. He heard footsteps in pursuit but saw no assailant. Disembodied laughter rang inside his head. He knew not for whom it tolled, or if it was a trick of the mind.

He ran till sweat soaked his undershirt. His ears hurt like there was something scuttling across the drum. Panting, he stumbled against a gnarled tree, which looked to have been split down the middle by a bolt of lightning. Wheezing, he saw a dark shape just ahead – obscured by trees and undergrowth.

A mud-log hut squatted in a clearing. He moved closer, towards a large tree stump in front of the dwelling. There was no firewood nor an axe in sight. The lower parts of the hut had sunk into the earth, as if being dragged towards the underworld. Its roof sagged, and the hovel eyed him with a single, shuttered window.

Light-headed, seeing stars, he gagged on a sickly-sweet smell. Close to emptying his stomach, he crept forward and pushed palm first against the crooked plank door – he gasped, not having seen the rusty nail, and instinctively squeezed the injured hand under his armpit.

Tugging off his torn glove, he winced at the painful red gash across his scaly palm, then shouldered the door a crack. Something blocked it from behind. He pushed again and heard its hinges creak. The door opened as far as it would go – and he slipped through the gap.

Inside, his boots squelched on the dirt floor. The sickly-sweet smell was replaced by one more rancid, as though a huntsman had gutted and skinned a stag. Water dripped from the ceiling into puddles. Moss and mushrooms speckled the walls. His eyes adjusted, and he discerned a mound of fallen straw beside the fireplace. There was a round, low-standing wooden table – he ran his fingers over the roughhewn tabletop. Many long, thin, overlapping cuts had been carved – hacked – into the sticky, darkened wood.

He saw a shadow on the floor – a coil of rope. And in the fireplace, a soiled garment... half-scorched. The Priest's purple stole.

"Now I have you," he said, but started at a sudden animal scream from outside. Frozen, he listened for many long seconds. *Must have been a fox.*

It screamed again. *No, not a fox.* Spying nothing through the gap between shutters, he peered closer, studying every copse and thicket. Had anything moved, it would have been too dark to see. Only a cat could have made anything out in that light – *a blacke cat…*

Breathing through his nose and shuddering, he crossed towards the door. Behind it stood a wooden barrel. It was the kind with which one churned butter. Its surface was darker and stickier than the tabletop. With his gloved hand, he nudged open the barrel lid, and immediately covered his mouth. *Oh God.*

He heaved open the door and fled outside but made it no further than the tree stump. A dark, motionless figure stood at the edge of the clearing. No, he was wrong, it was a shadow cast by the trees. But surely it was a cloaked, hooded figure? No, it had to be an illusion, a trick of the light. The figure cradled something in its arms – nothing more than the crook of a tree limb…

He heard that sound again, that scream. *Not a fox.* So he ran for the trees, but then slipped in a patch of mud and went flying. Landing face first, his head hit an exposed root as he slid across the floor. Groaning, he held his head and released a slow, pained breath.

Above him, a spider web was strung between two branches – a thousand stuck droplets of dew glistening in the moonlight. He brushed nettles with his bare hand and recoiled. A cluster of berries dangled from a weed-like plant. Starved, almost rabid, he tore off as many as he could and wolfed them down.

Gnashing on them, feeling them burst between his teeth, sweet, tart juices running down his chin, he was, for a moment, in ecstasy, on a bed of gold and silver, with beautiful women… buxom blonde Scandinavian women! Mermaids crowned with seashells! Slippery wet scales alive with tiny iridescent crustaceans. Mermaids with heaving, slippery bosoms the likes of which he'd never imagined – and then the taste turned bitter, pungent and sticky, like chomping on rotten figs.

He spied an old crone, some bent old hag stirring a humungous black pot, her long matted hair trailing like a horse's mane over her flabby naked backside. Bats and snakes were biting at her bloody nipples, breasts dried up and sagging like empty flour sacks. Stirring, stirring with an old bone, cackling toothlessly – *Ha-ha-ha-ha-ha!* – flames tickling him, cooking him as his own burnt flesh smell wafted up to his nostrils – *Patooh* – he spat out the berries.

Flapping from lip to lip, his limp foamy tongue slithered inside his mouth. He inhaled as deeply as his stuffy nose could manage. Snot bubbled and burst as he exhaled – croaked out a gurgling, sticky cough. *So much bloode...*

Head pounding. That sound, was it true? Splashing on rocks in his ear. *So thirsty.* He felt it in the earth – a river running between its banks over his skin... *Back to the village – escape, yes, flee, go, Matthew. Take the money and run, like alwayes...* Crunching leaves, snapping twigs. A dream of water. Earth moving beneath him. Dream too loud, hands in the dirt, clawing up the soil. Tumbling – *Ow!* – rolling over rocks. *SPLASH.* So cold! Where was his hat? "Mubber," he gurgled, "bliz-blab-yoo?"

***

IV

Matthew wyped His Nose on His Shirt cv *f f*. Grey Clowdes kepte ovt the Svn so that No one caste a Shadowe in the crowded Sqvare. His *f*eete sqvelched in the Pvddles that ran *f*rom o'er *f*lowing Pits o*f f*est'ring wayst, as Labovrers shovelled Horseshit and Hvman excremente into a carte *f*illed with haye. Svmmer's *f*ar-o*f f* stenche was bvt a lingering memorie, the Colde weather a blessing to the nostrils.

She was so very, very Layte. It was getting Colder every minvte. How long vntil She arrived? From which direction wovld She appeare?

"I 'eard She blvdgeoned Him while He slepte," saide the ayproned Flesher, brandishing an invisible Hammer.

An able Seaman stamped His wooden Leg. "Only in My worst imagynings... E'er svch a *f*ancie Woman stepped aboarde My Vessel, I'd 'avl Her o*f f* Shippe and down into the saltie Bryne belowe."

"Aye, and no one wovld 'old yov t'accownte."

"Aye," the Seaman saide.

"Aye. And nowe 'ere we 're withowt a Blacksmyth."

The Sailor nodded, as i*f* to saye, *Aye, t'is trve, t'is trve.*

Her laste wordes still havnted Him. Hidden beneathe Her bedde, Bloode still drying on His *f*ingernails. "Yov'll see Me againe, My Love. Don't worrie."

The Clowdes parted and bayde the Svn streame downe on the dirt Sqvare. Dazzled, Matthew sqvinted, and stepped into the Shadowe o*f* the Gallowes. The Noose was plaine to see, thovgh it dangled Twelve *f*eete o*f f* the grownde. Its Shadowe dri*f*ted to and *f*ro, like Re*f*vse cavght in a River's cvrrente.

"Terryble, terryble, terryble," saide the Haberdasher's wy*f*e, shaking Her heade. "And what will become o*f* Her children?"

"That babbie Girl o*f* Hers dyed Months back," saide the Cobbler's davghter. "Sicke *f*rom the daye it'd beene Borne. One daye, it jvst didn't wayke vp."

Behynd the Gallowes loomed the Prison. He wrvng His handes jvst looking at it. Portcvllis down, all was Darke wythin, qviet bvt *f*or the hal*f*-heard Whispers and Moanes and the clanging o*f* cayge Doores that only He covld heare.

"What abovt that Boye o*f* Hers?"

"That little Rvnt? He creepes lyke the Devil. No one can *f*ind Him – ran o*f f* God knowswhere—"

The Alewy*f*e gasped, and then *f*aynted, at the syght o*f* a cloaked Ryder on a Blacke Horse. Eyes wyld, bitte drypping *f*oame, the Horse reared vp on its backe Legges, whynnying, and dryving its Hooves. The Ryder, in His cloake and capotain, myght have beene mistaken *f*or a Hyghwayman.

All *f*ell sylent as He spowke: "Harke! All Yov God-*f*earing *f*olke, I bidde Yov listen. My nayme is Jeremyah Hopkins, and I be a Wytch*f*ynder…

"One o*f* Yovr owne standes accvsed o*f* slaying Her hvsbande… She be mowst certainlie Damned. Marke me, svch Crymes are not vnhearde o*f* amonge Civilysed People. Per'aps He beate Her once too o*f*ten. Per'aps She meante to vsvrpe Him o*f* all His coyn and absconde. Or per'aps there be *another* motive…"

Hopkins swepte over the Crowde with His gayze. Eyes madde with Fvrie – voyce calme and controlled. "I pvt it to Yov that She sygned Her Nayme in the Unholie Booke.

"Yea, according to Tests devysed by ovr King, We dvnked Her in yonder River, and yet She *re f vsed* to sinke. I, mysel*f*, pricked Her with this Needle, and She did not Bleede. And that which She claymed to be a hvmble Birthmarke, I saye, be nothing lesse than a Marke o*f* the Beaste. I saye … She be a Wytch!"

The Crowde jostled and jeered at the very Worde. Stray elbowes knocked Matthew downe into the mvdde – all arownd Him a Sea o*f* Bootes and Clogges, ragged Skirtes and *f*ilthie Pantaloones. Handes in the dirt, He wyped awaye the teares with the backe o*f* His wriste, when two tall Blacke spvrred Bootes planted themselves be*f*ore Him.

Hopkins hawled Him vp by the Armpits. "On Yovr *f*eete, Boye," the Wytch*f*ynder saide – He mvste have beene three tymes His Senior and wore a bobbe o ƒ Blacke Haire downe to the Shovlders. Eyes lyke a Birde o ƒ Preye.

"Tell Me, Ladde, is She Yovr Mother?" He saide, twisting Matthew's wryst. Hopkins' long Arms seemed too long, even ƒor svch a slender Frayme. "Yov know what She is then, don't Yov? I praye God be Merci ƒvll on Her, Boye."

Matthew sqvirmed. "Let go o ƒ Me!" He cryed, and ƒell backe in the mvdde.

"What is to be donne with svch a Woman that depryves Her chyld o ƒ His Father?"

The Crowde booed againe. "Hang Her! Bring Her ovte and Hang Her!" The Alehovse Keeper, holding His wy ƒe steadie, cvpped one Hande and called, "We wishe to 'eare no more conjectvre, 'opkins. Ovr Croppes have ƒayled. Dysease a ƒ ƒlictes ovr Lyvestocke. She cannot be sv ƒ ƒered to Live."

The Wytch ƒynder looked down His Nose. "Very well. Let vs pvtte it to Bedde." He nodded to the Blacke-hooded Hangman, who then marched over to the Prison and called inside. Chayns clinked and coyled behynd the Gayte, vntil, ƒvlly raysed, the Portcvllis disappeared, leaving novght bvt Teethe in its Mowthe. And ƒrom the Darknesse wythin, there She appeared, Eye Blackened, lovelie Redde Haire dyshevelled and matted beneathe Her coi ƒ.

"Whore!" "Jezebel!" "Wytch!" the Towns ƒolke yelled, tossing rotten apples. He called ovt to Her, bvt His Voyce was so smalle, He covld hardlie heare Himsel ƒ over the jeering Crowde.

Ledde by the Hangman to the Gallowes, She whimpered as He tore o ƒ ƒ Her coi ƒ and tyghtened the Noose arownd Her Necke. "Madeleine Procter," Hopkins saide. "Yov stande accvsed o ƒ Heresie, Diabolysm, Wytchcra ƒt, and In ƒanticyde."

Handes bovnde behynd Her backe, She raysed Her heade to the Skye, and croaked, "I didn't do it. Lorde have Mercie, I am not Gviltie."

"Yov will hang by the Necke vntil Yov are Deade."

When She saw Him, mvddied and shyvering and watching *f*rom the Crowde, She opened Her Mowthe to screame. Then the *f*loore dropt.

The rope cracked and twysted vnder the svdden pressvre, Her Bodie swaying, Eyes bvlging, as She gasped *f*or aire. Her Necke hadn't broken.

The Towns*f*olke roared with lavghter as She kicked Her Legges and *f*lowndered: "Looke, She's swymming!" "What a syght!" "Thinks She's a Mermayde!"

All He covld do was watch as She clvng to Breath. Tyme seemed to halte. Until the Hangman cvt Her loose.

She hit the Grownde at an odd angle, snapping Her ankle. Handes still bownde, She screamed into the dirt. The wooden steppes descending the Gallowes creaked vnder the Hangman's weyght, *f*ollowed by a greyt metallick *THUMP-THUMP-THUMP*.

"No, no, no," She cryed as the Hangman approwched, bvt it was vseless – the Shovel was already vpon Her. *CLANG*… *CLANG*… *CLANG*… He went to deliver a *f*ovrth Heade blowe bvt *f*ayled to *f*ollowe throvgh.

Matthew opened His eyes. The Wytch*f*ynder loomed over Him. "Yov can't helpe Her nowe, Boye. Yov can ownly helpe Yovrsel*f*. Come with Me and Yov'll be doing God's worke."

He didn't lysten. "Mother, Mother, Mother," He saide, sqveezing Her lyke He'd always done, *f*or as long as He'd lived. She smelled the sayme even now. In His Mynd, He saw Svn*f*lowers and *f*resh-bayked Breade.

Cheeke to His Mother's Cheeke, He shvt His Eyes as some Townswoman showted, "Hang Him too! Pvt an ende to that She-Devil's Bloodelyne!" The Crowde roared their approbation, bvt Hopkins halted the Stampeede – Arms akimbo as i*f* to Martyr Himsel*f* on the spotte. "This Boye shall be an example o*f* God's Almyghtie Jvstyce and nothing lesse.

"Rescved *f*rom Heathenry, He has beene given a seconde chance. And whether He lykes it or not... He's coming with Me."

✳✳✳

V

Water tugged at his boots – no feeling in his toes. A feeling of falling. Fairies and white-spotted fawns frolicked, he'd heard, in glittering woodland ponds. He heard them, still, calling his name – a dream of Mermaids. *O heare their Siren calle!*

Half-conscious and chuckling to himself – *Come here, you Beauties; you want a reale Man? Take a looke at this!* – he reached beneath his waistband and – "Argh!" – out flopped a brown spotted fish. Somersaulting – *SMACK* – onto the pebbles, the trout flapped wetly, its scales shimmering iridescently in the cloudy light. Then it stopped flapping.

Matthew squinted and rolled over onto his belly. Wreathed by clouds, the pale sun streamed down over the great waves of foliage over the labyrinthine woods. Tiny flies circled and darted through the air. Cheek down against the pebbled riverbank, he listened as it ruffled its wings and pecked at a mossy green boulder. Sight fogged as if by steam, he knew it to be a Crow, although it remained to him a blurry fluttering black thing. And propped up against the rock—

"Smithy!" he croaked, spitting blood and berry juice. The red stuff trickled away, coating the pebbles like ink. *"Smithy?"* There was a wrenching pain in his bowels, and bile crept up into his throat. No, no, he absolutely would not soil himself...

Smithy gurgled.

"Smithy, t'is me. Matthew." He crawled closer, right arm limp and tingling, unable to make out the Boy's face. "Speake, Smithy." He patted the Boy's hand, in which was clutched a tuft of—*Red haire... But I saw her hang!*

The Crow hopped from foot to foot, dangling something from its beak that wriggled like a freshly plucked worm.

Matthew reached forward half-blindly, aiming to plant his hand on Smithy's shoulder – "Speake, Smithy, *speake*" – but, instead, poked his finger into a cold wet hollow in the Boy's face.

CAW-CAW-CAW! Matthew launched himself backwards onto a half-buried rock. Curled up in pain like a poked slug, his vision cleared, and he saw it – the red stalk of Smithy's eyeball dangling from the Crow's beak.

The Bird guzzled down the Boy's eye and started pecking at his nose. Matthew tossed a pebble, striking the vermin down, whereupon he grabbed it by the legs and, bounding berserker-like over the riverbank, heaved it flapping into the water. Cawing madly, the Bird failed to escape the current and was washed away into the wilderness. He followed it out of sight, listening to the river sloshing against its banks, and in his mind, he traced his path and followed the wend of the water beyond the trees – to where he knew the village waited.

***

Matthew brushed away the leaves from his face. Peeking out from a dense thicket, he spied the Innkeeper and Blacksmyth conferring outside the church. He waited and listened. "Damn, where is he?" asked the grizzled Blacksmyth. "He's holding the whole thing up."

What were they talking aboute? *Some Diabolical blacke mass inside the church? In broade daylight, no less…*

"He can't have gone far," said the Innkeeper. "But we better find him quick." The two men marched off in opposite directions through the trees.

Matthew waited, watching, lest they return. *This conspiracie has to be exposed – and I will be the one to do it! The Priest is the keye to it all, a Wolfe disguised as Shepherde – leading the flocke astraye. Or are they Wytches, all of them? The whole village must have beene in on the charade. I could flee… But then again, I am no coward. All I need is a signe upon which to acte…*

"Where am I?" asked Garrick Hardwood, squinting, as he stumbled out of the undergrowth. The old man, in his best doublet and boots, tapped his stick along the floor, only to stop, reach one hand into his hoes and piss up the wall of the church. Shaking off, he then hobbled towards the entrance, but not before Matthew wrested his stick away and knocked him on the side of the head. The old man crumpled, whereupon Matthew dragged him into a bush.

He listened at the church doors – ominous chanting emanated from within. There had to be another way – take them by surprise. Running low, Matthew half-circled to the back and found the Priest's entrance. He tried the rusty iron handle, heard the latch creak – it opened!

The Priest's voice slowly came into earshot as he approached the curtained passageway. Peeking out, he saw the Priest standing at the altar with… Belinda, the innkeeper's daughter? She wore a white dress and a crown of daffodils. She had her arms folded across her chest like a sulking child.

"Please remain seated, everyone," said the Priest. "The Groome, it seems, has wandered off. I'm sure he'll return shortly, whereupon we shall recommence the ceremonie…"

Of course, it made perfect sense. They were marrying Belinda off to the Dark Lord. He might have known the village folk were up to no good. No matter, for now was his chance to expose the conspiracy before it reached its endgame. At last, God was with him!

He sprang out from behind the curtain and with a finger accused the Priest: "Now, I have you!" The crowd of wedding guests gasped, some leaping up out of their seats. The Blacksmyth and Innkeeper looked on and scratched their heads.

Father Nicholas spun around. "Oh, not you againe."

Belinda followed suit. "Mr Wytchfynder?"

He held out his hand to her as he pushed past Father Nicholas. "I'm here to rescue you, Belinda. Have courage, childe, I shall snatch you from the Forces of Darknesse. For I am a Wytchfynder!"

The Priest shook his head. "Have you gone madde, man? This is a wedding!"

"That's what you'd like me to think… Alas, no, t'is a Conspiracie." Here he turned to the guests seated in the pews. "And this so-called Priest is its Chiefe Architect. Yea, Goode People, I entered the Lion's Den and survived. But my poore Smithy shall not have suffered in vaine. The Lord shall smite mine enemies!"

The Priest put up his hands. "Do not listen to this foole. He has clearly gone madde in the heade."

Matthew cackled. "Lies. I found your hovel in the woodes, Father Nicholas. I saw the stole you tried to burne. T'is you who's responsible for the missing children! Think yourself some Gilles-de-Rais? I am wise to your crimes."

The Priest half-laughed, then cleared his throat. "T'is not the time or place to be conducting your obscene investigations. Tell us, where be this stole of mine you *claime* to have founde?"

Matthew hesitated. Damn! He must have lost it in the woodes. "You meane to vex me. I put it to you all that this be an unholie union between Belinda – and he whom you all now serve – your Master Satan!"

"Oh, my heade, swing a donkey by the bollocks!" said Garrick Hardwood as he stumbled inside.

"Darling!" cried Belinda, lifting her skirts as she hurried into his waiting arms, and then slapped his chest. "Where have you been, you olde foole?"

Garrick kissed her wetly on the mouth, tongue and all, and then pointed his stick at Matthew. "I only went for a slashe, Love, and *this one* knockes me on the backe of the heade— Gorblimey, look at that arme of his! T'is crimson as a Dæmon's haemorrhoides."

Matthew shrieked, for somewhere his sleeve had been torn, and his entire forearm had been replaced by some Stygian appendage. Yellow pus seeped from every leathery wrinkle and sore. His knees grew weak, and he steadied himself against the baptismal font. He held his red arm to his chest like a leper.

The Priest crossed himself. "T'is the Devil's right hand. He is marked by the Beaste."

Matthew shook his head. "Nonsense, lies, I was stung by nettles." He brandished his scaly claw at anyone who approached. "I ate some berries—" He clutched his stomach as a sudden sharp pain doubled him over, and then spewed pea-green vomit into the face of the Priest.

Father Nicholas, blinking away the dripping soup, spluttered and retched, before stuttering, "He-he-he's possessed! God helpe us, he's the Devil's Servant!"

"What? No!" Hands on his hips. "Harke, all you God-fearing folke! You will not keepe me from—" He spewed up again, this time all over Belinda. She screamed, powerless to stop the green deluge that utterly drenched her.

The Priest pointed one crooked, trembling finger. "Somebody stoppe him, he's a danger to us all!"

"He had me hange my lovelie Daughter-in-Law!" said the

Blacksmyth.

"His clothes are too cleane!" said the Milkmaid's Daughter.

"His haire is curlie like the Devil's!" said the Alewife.

"He's had uncleane thoughts aboute our Daughter Belinda," said the Innkeeper. "And now he meanes to spoile her wedding daye!"

Hardwood piped up again. "I saw him fornicating in the woodes with a cottonwood tree!"

And all at once they were upon him. Curses flying like carrion birds, legs kicking like mules. Someone chucked their boot at his head. He parried lamely with his good arm, until a hairy fist connected – *SMACK* – against his cheek. He went down – bruised and cracked – felt his head scatter like dropped coins. Then… all the villagers stood back.

"Well? What are you waiting for?" he said. "Martyr me, you Heathen fooles!" No response. A sea of contemplative eyes, they waited, hands by their sides. *Dumb country folke*. Quick on his feet, eyes over the shoulder, he hobbled towards the exit. *Flee, steale a horse, go backe to civilisation*. One glance over his shoulder, and then ahead, to where the sun was streaming down – flooding the doorway with celestial light. *God is with me*… Only then did he see the flat side of a shovel rushing towards his face.

VI

Dreaming of apples and fresh-baked bread, Matthew felt the wind on his face. It whistled past his ears as, half-asleep, he opened his eyes, and squinted. A yellow sun was rising over the horizon, the long slope of the hill ran down towards the village, and beyond that, the great wild of Albion stretched out into eternity.

Squirming against the rope that held him fast to the oak tree on the hill, straw scratched at his freezing toes. Left and right, felled branches and wood logs were propped up against the tree… And above his head was the twisted bough where—

A Crow hopped out from the foliage. It peered at him with its beady black eye, and then was upon him, a flurry of flapping wings and talons. His cheeks ran red as it fluttered and came to rest on his shoulder. He shrugged it off, but the Bird hopped over his head and tugged at his earlobe, pecking it like a worm out of the ground.

"Oh God, oh God, absolve me," he cried, thrashing, as the Bird pecked him again and again. Eyes squeezed shut, he felt the blood trickling down his neck – until his earlobe finally tore away. He shrieked and shook his head, but then – a sudden dart of pain and a cold wet feeling where his left eye should have been. Wings fluttered, he saw the ground; the Bird cawed, the ground disappeared.

The Crow guzzled down his eyeball, red wormy stalk and all, and he couldn't help but laugh when it hopped onto his head and dug its talons into his scalp. The sudden crackle of ignition might have been a cause for concern for some country lout, but here he was, an educated man, at last wholly certain of his place in the universe – no less certain, in fact, than the sudden warmth tickling his feet. No, nothing could stop him laughing – for he knew now that God was with him. Had his arms not been bound he would have tossed them akimbo in utter martyrdom.

"I am UNTOUCHABLE," he declaimed, and the Crow, in answer, chuckled and then laughed with all the cadence of a woman's voice. Peering at him upside down, and eyeing his one remaining eye, the Bird cawed and said, "You, Sir, are in a Heape of Trouble."

Heart's Desire

by Michael Victor Bowman

Starling was carving runes into the bleached bone of a man's upper arm when there was an urgent knocking on the door. Shocked by the sound, she dropped the bone and her small blade into the embers of the fire. But instead of complaining, she yipped with delight and bounced up off her stool, excited by the thought of a visitor. Who could it be? she wondered, as she twitched her deep hood over her head. Perhaps a farmer in search of a blessing for his harvest? And she smiled at the thought of the trinkets he would have brought in trade. Or maybe it was the village maid who kept falling for that young boy's charms? She often came to Starling for a potion to remedy her dishonour and escape the wrath of her father. As she approached the door, she paused to adjust her long cloak over her shoulders, savouring the moment of anticipation. Tugging her hood down, she unlatched the door and pulled it open.

The bright sun glared off polished metal. Blinded, she stepped back, unwittingly saving her own life; the point of a sword flashed across her throat, the vicious tip only nicking the flesh instead of severing her head. She didn't even have time to scream: couldn't spare the breath as she scrambled backwards, tripping over the fire, tipping the cooking pot over in a shower of sparks as the enormous, hulking shadow of her assailant pursued her into her home. She didn't see the next blow coming, she sensed it and in desperation grabbed her stool and thrust it out before her. She felt the sword chop into it, the force of the impact nearly tearing her makeshift shield from her hands. But she recovered in time to intercept the next blow, and the next. Her attacker hefted his short but heavy weapon with ease and scythed down onto the stool again and again, carving the frail wooden furniture into fragments. In seconds there was nothing left but two lengths of wood, and she threw them at her attacker's head before turning to run once again.

But she didn't get far. He was bigger, stronger, faster and he had her pinned against the back wall of her little cottage, had his enormous forearm pressed into her back, squeezing the air out of her slight and slender frame. Then she felt the angry tip of his sword work past the fabric of her collar and prick the exposed skin between her shoulder and clavicle, ready to thrust down through her chest cavity, to slice through her lungs and tear a gaping wound right through her heart. She would be dead in an instant. The odour of musky sweat and strong ale filled her nose as he leant closer into her. She clenched her teeth as she felt him press himself against the back of her thighs. Was this what he had come for? Was this how her life would end? But then hot alcoholic breath bathed the side of her face as a voice like a rock slide growled, 'Where is it?'

She forced herself to swallow and, tremulously, asked, 'Where's what?'

It was the wrong thing to say. The point of the sword left her flesh and the fist that held it smashed into the brittle white plaster of the wall beside her head, showering her in fragments. This time she screamed, but was choked off by the other hand that gripped her throat, spun her around and slammed her back against the wall. In the same moment, her attacker gave vent to a terrifying war cry, so loud it seemed it must shake the rough hewn rafters, and rattle the pots and jars that hung from them. Terrifying, or terrified? Because now she could see his eyes as he levelled his sword at her face. She could look back at him along the shaking length of his steel blade and see the paling skin, the gaping mouth and the widening eyes. And in the same moment she realised why. Her hood had slipped off. She was exposed.

'Gods preserve me,' he breathed. 'It's true!'

His moment of hesitation was all that Starling needed. She reached up to the hand that choked her and raked her long nails across the intruder's forearm. They bit as deep as claws and, as the flesh tore open, he howled in pain. Starling twisted out of his weakened grip and scrurried around the edge of the room. Now she had the initiative and, as the man swung his weapon, she danced out of range on her agile, naked feet, bounced like a pole vaulter at the Summer Games and leapt up towards the roof, her back arching as one slender arm thrust upwards. Her long-nailed hand closed on the haft of an elegant bronze sword hidden in the depth of thatch, above. Landing in a crouch, she whipped the sword around in a wide arc at knee height. The tip of her leaf-shaped blade sliced through the flesh of the man's naked thigh and he roared again. Now, canines flashing and mouth gaping like a predator anticipating the first taste of blood, she raised her sword two-handed, gave vent to a warbling cry, and slashed down at his head.

But the man parried Starling's blow with practised ease. Almost in the same instant he rolled his wrist and cracked his brutal weapon down onto the flat of her ornate blade. Tempered steel met burnished bronze and the bronze blade clattered to the floor, leaving the mortified Starling just a few inches of metal protruding from her hands.

The intruder grinned at her through his grimace of pain

and let fly with his sword once more. But Starling was still too quick for him and she dodged, floating backwards out of range, her robe billowing about her like a cloud. She had lost her weapon, but she wasn't worried. The poisoned edge of her ancient blade would soon do its work. She had the advantage now. Skipping lightly across the room, she slammed the door closed once more and spun around to face her would-be molester, arms and legs spread wide as though to bar his way.

The dust settled and, for a moment, only the sound of their gasps could be heard, like two lovers who had paused to rest between the sheets. Starling grinned at her opponent. Blood poured down his left arm and over his hand from the deep gouges she had rent with her nails. More blood wept from the red mouth she had opened in the bulge of his right thigh, dribbling in tracks down his leg and into his soft leather boot. A grass-stained tunic clad his torso, beneath which hung the trademark skirt of chain and leather that marked him out as a soldier, as if the close-cropped scalp were not evidence enough. Yet this man was not entirely civilised: there was still the strong stink of barbarian about him in the elaborate circular tattoos that adorned his arms and crept up the sides of his neck. They hinted at the more impressive body art that must lie hidden beneath his tunic, that must curl across his chest like eddies in a forest pool, and ripple down his muscled torso like fresh spring water cascading over stones... Starling found herself licking her lips and, horrified, quickly checked her savage impulses with a silent reprimand. Control yourself! By the gods, she had slept alone too long.

But if there was any attraction between them, it was one-sided.

'Dog-faced bitch!' the soldier spat, his fear now replaced by revulsion.

Starling laughed maniacally. 'Is that supposed to offend

me?' But even so, she raised her hood once more and hid her face in its shadow.

'Where is it?' he roared, staggering closer.

'Where's what?' Starling asked again, slinking sideways along the wall to keep the distance between them.

The soldier shook his head as though trying to clear it, sending out a shower of sweat like a wet dog. He levelled his sword at Starling and gave her a hard stare. 'Where are the bones of the oracle?' he demanded. 'Where is the head of Death? Quickly, woman! Or I will carve you into steaks and find it myself.'

'I know nothing of a death's head! How dare you attack me, you filthy, pig-groping son of a whore! If anyone is to be carved up it will be you! You stinking, wine-soaked, sun-addled lech!'

'Witch!' he shouted hoarsely and swiped at her with his sword, but his arm was weakened, the stroke enfeebled: the weapon struck the dusty ground with a dull ring and he had not the strength to lift it again.

Starling giggled. 'You will soon bleed to death, slave,' she whispered, crouching against the wall. The soldier struggled to keep his feet with one lame leg as his life spread darkly across Starling's floor. 'My blade poisoned you,' she added, almost conversationally. 'See how your blood flows? Your wounds are small but they will drain you dry.'

The soldier's drawn face contorted as his chest heaved for breath. 'Why do you call me slave?' he gasped.

'Because you serve the King,' Starling replied. 'He who promises much but delivers little. You are a slave. But you were once free, I see,' she replied as her eyes traced the elaborate intertwining tattoos.

'Lies! Riddles!' He heaved between rapid breaths. 'Fight me, but do not spin your charms to undo my mind!' As Starling watched, his good leg finally buckled at the knee and he sank with a wet thud onto the swept earth that was made mud by his own blood. His face twisted with pain and Starling found that she had to look away. The red heat and high spirits of battle had cooled and in the shivering aftermath she was discovering that she was not the killer she had always imagined herself to be.

Whenever she had walked abroad she had always comforted herself with thoughts of how dangerous she could be. When she had seen men on the road, or passed through a village and felt many eyes upon her, she had steeled herself by imagining how fierce she would be in battle, how ruthlessly she would dispatch her attackers, and how savage would be her satisfaction as she delivered natural justice to those who had dared assault her. And now, it had finally happened: her moment of reckoning! For the first time in her eighteen years she had faced mortal danger and she had prevailed! A part of her was glad of that, but the greater part felt sorrow as she watched the soldier fade away. Need it have come to this? Need she have fought him? He was obviously drunk. Perhaps he was simply parted from his wits by strong ale and too long at the front without women?

But he had demanded the Death's Head.

There was more to this than unsated urges. But what, she might never know. He must have drunk deeply before coming here. Enough ale could dampen the poison for a little while, but soon it would do its work. His lids were already closing, his eyes rolling back in his head. She rose from her crouch and stalked towards the man. She must have answers before he died!

***

Night fell and the cottage darkened. A single candle guttered, flickering in Braega's glazed eyes as his wits returned to him. He tried to swallow, but his mouth was as dry as a cotton sack. He tried to move, but his body was heavy like dead meat. As he slowly regained his senses, he realised that he lay upon a wooden cot: he could feel its narrow frame pinching him like a tight-fitting coffin, while beneath him the taught cloth that stretched across it was bowed beneath the weight of his body. His right hand rested at his side, while the injured left was draped across his chest. There was a wetness at the top of his right thigh, and the smell of blood was strong in the warm, fetid air. His wounds were tightly bound, so tightly that his lower leg was almost numb, as was his left forearm.

He turned his head and, through the haze of his half-closed eyes, he dimly saw the far wall of the cottage. A primitive hovel it was: a round hut made of mud and straw plastered onto a crude wicker frame, the staves of which showed through in places where the ancient plaster had cracked. Clearly this wild woman was no builder, for the place was dearly in need of repair. But she was an artist of sorts, for it was not the decrepit state of the cottage which drew Braega's attention, but the elaborate drawings scratched into the mud of the walls, drawings which covered that curved brown canvas in a sea of monsters and myths. Across the wall pranced headless beings with faces in their chests. They were joined by monopedal dwarves with tusks protruding from their snarling mouths, while above them flew a winged lion with the barbed tail of a scorpion. Giant insects with ghostly human faces stalked below, harried by a snake-like flying creature with the head and horns of a bull. These and many more strange, terrifying, inhuman figures cavorted in the candlelight around him as though alive, as though all the haunting childhood tales he had ever heard had come to life.

The scrape of a foot on the compacted dirt floor alerted him to her presence. Braega quickly closed his eyes and lay back. Listening hard, he heard the rustle of her garment, the clack of pottery and the barely detectable pad of her bare feet as she approached him. It was all he could do to remain still. What torture had she planned? Why had she tended his wounds if not to prolong his agony? Perhaps, after her pleasure, the cooking pot awaited him. But she was a fool: she had not chained him, relying instead on whatever charm had lulled him to sleep. When she came closer, he would have her. Surprise would be his weapon, as it had been when he burst through the door. But he must wait until she was close.

Something hard and blunt stabbed into his chest, right below the sternum. His eyes bulged open, his mouth gaping wide as the wind was driven from his lungs. The black pit of the witch's hood hovered just above his face as she crouched like a predator straddling its prey, one knee pressed down into his chest where she had landed after her flying leap from across the floor, for it was now her turn to surprise him! As he wheezed she raised her mixing bowl and poured its thick, warm, yellow contents into his gaping, breathless mouth. He heard the sound of her girlish giggle as it hit the back of his throat, causing him to cough and choke. But down it went like thick, hot sludge and he fell back upon the cot, spent and gasping.

Unhurried, the witch climbed down and patted him on the shoulder. 'There, there,' she soothed. 'Did the big, brave warrior get a taste of his own medicine?' And she giggled again.

'By the gods,' he croaked, grimacing. 'What was that?'

'It is my elixir. It will heal you.'

'What is in it?'

'Oh, elderberry, stewed apple, my water.'

Braega blinked. 'Your water?'

'Of course. Shamanism is a magic of the body.' And as realisation dawned across his face and rage coloured it, she giggled again, easily dodging his clumsy lunge as he tried to grab her. Still giggling, she returned to his bedside and sat on the edge of the cot, legs crossed and arms folded easily in her lap. 'Did you not know that?' she teased.

He uttered something foul which only provoked her laughter once more. 'Witch!' he exploded. 'You have no honour! You toy with men, weave your charms and poison them with your excrement. But you hide your face in shame for you are an unnatural thing. Know this: others are coming and they will make an end of you!' He ended in a fit of dry coughing and fell back onto the mean bed, exhausted again.

Starling sobered. She gazed down at the man and nodded. 'Yes, I have poisoned you, warrior, but not with my elixir. You should be grateful! My waters will null the toxin from my blade until your strength returns.'

Braega scowled. 'To what purpose? What do you want of me? A slave? A plaything for your tortures? A fresh meal?'

But Starling did not answer. In the feeble candlelight, her face was still hidden beneath the hood: the face that Braega had already glimpsed. But he had already begun to question the memory, to dismiss it as a cunning trick. For surely it was a deception? As she sat beside him, her robe fell away to reveal the slim and shapely legs of a young maid... a human maid. And as she had straddled the cot to pour her foul issue down his gullet, he had not failed to notice the comely naked torso that had flashed briefly in the candlelight. No, ale and anguish must be clouding his mind. 'I do not fear you,' he muttered, disdainfully. 'Go back to your village, girl, and give up these games. You are no half-human shaman. No such exists in the world of men.'

Starling made no reply. Instead, she bowed her head as though acknowledging the truth, but then reached up with her long-nailed hands and flicked her hood back. Feeble as the candle was, there was no denying what Braega saw. The predatory face of a wolf looked down upon him. Pointed ears, ash grey fur and eyes that were tinged with blue behind deep black pupils that looked at him, into him and through him. He could not hold their gaze for long.

'It's true,' he whispered in awe. 'Dog head!'

Starling sighed. 'You have travelled too long in the realm of the King, warrior of the forest tribe, and have forgotten the lessons of your people.'

'What do you want of me?' he repeated, but this time a little fearfully.

'Why do you seek the Death's Head?' she asked him.

His face darkened and he looked away.

'Why do you seek to know that which no man should know?'

Braega might have told the witch what she could do with her questions, but he was growing so tired it was almost too much effort to breathe. His head suddenly felt so heavy it was all he could do to turn it on the thin, straw pillow. His body felt numb and cold. Beneath the bandages his arm and leg no longer pulsed warmly, but felt as dead as the blade of his sword. He looked past the shaman, his eyes drawn to the candlelight, but as he tried to focus on the flame his vision began to blur and he realised he was beginning to slip away. He was dying! In a panic he reached out with his good arm like a drowning man, grasping the arm of the witch who sat before him. But rather than tear free of him, she took his hand in hers and said soothingly, 'Hush... hush... I know, I know.'

But he must tell her... if he were truly dying, she must know the rituals of his people. He must be laid out beneath the moon so that the Goddess could take him to the afterlife, or his soul would be lost forever! He fought to keep his eyes open, to blink away the creeping shadows that spread across his sight like blood through water. But his vision faded and his mind drifted on torpid currents through winding mists while a voice whispered to him. 'Now, warrior of the forest tribe, you will dream. You will dream and tell me your secrets. Why have you come here? Where have you come from? And why do you desire Death's head?'

∗∗∗

For twenty-five years Braega's solitary existence had not bothered him. Not, that is, until the day before his discharge, the day he and his comrades had sat and talked of what would come and he had realised, in an awful moment of clarity, that he was the only one who had no home to go to. Every man around him had, if not children, at least a wife waiting somewhere. How had they done this? Braega had wondered. How had they found the time? And suddenly, twenty-five years felt not like a triumph but a death sentence, and he had gone from the happy, chatty breakfast table straight to his tent and the bottle. There, he had brooded on the availability of women until a hot hatred of married men had ignited in his gut. Then he had turned his intoxicated eyes on the glittering tent of his commander wherein the Commandant's wife reclined. She was middle-aged, but she was firm and she'd have been better than nothing. But even drunk and desperate, he could not take a woman against her will and had paused at the threshold, staring at her as though stupefied while she stared back at him in terror. As he had retreated in shame she had cried out and drawn the Commandant's Guard. But if twenty-five years on the frontlines doesn't get you a wife, it does develop reflexes that work even when the mind behind them is relieved of its senses. And so it was that he had woken up in a forest glade, miles from camp and with one of the guards' swords still clutched in his hand, and the blade still wet with blood.

In this distant corner of a barbarian land he had experienced his second awful realisation of the day: that he had just thrown away his twenty-five years of loyal service to the King and had trashed his chances of citizenship, a home and a family, forever. As he knelt in the bracken he knew that all was lost. Only one thing remained and so, with great solemnity, he had slowly raised the sword with both hands, felt the point of it press into his chest, closed his eyes and drawn his last breath.

'No, Braega!'

Braega looked down to see his father's big, tanned brown hand reach down over his shoulder and wrap itself around both of his as they clasped the… chisel? He stared dumbly at the tool which he held towards him, while before him now rested an unfinished carving wrought from a rough-hewn log. 'Not like that,' the voice said, and Braega turned and looked up into a face he had not seen for twenty-five years and never thought to see again, for his father was dead. 'Never turn a blade towards yourself,' his father explained, and smiled.

'Father!' Braega cried.

'What is it that you want, son?' his father asked.

'I want to come home!' Braega answered, childish tears welling up in his eyes.

But his father shook his head. 'You cannot,' he replied. 'If you die a soldier's death, you will doom your soul forever. You are not a man of the King's realm, Braega. You are one of us. Among our people a man's afterlife is determined by the manner of his ending. If you die by the sword, you will not know peace, and we will not meet again in the hereafter.'

'But there is nothing left to me, father. The King's men are coming. I will either die at their hands, or my own.'

The apparition was silent for a moment, its face creasing with anxiety, an expression Braega did not remember ever seeing on his father's face in life. Presently, it spoke again. 'Do you remember the story of the oracles?'

Braega nodded.

'Among their kind was one known as the oracle of death, whose severed head retained the power to grant a man a vision of his destiny. Before you end your life on the point of a sword, seek out the head of Death and see the fate you would so quickly embrace, for I know it is not your heart's desire, Braega. You were not born to be a warrior.'

'The oracles? They are just a myth!' Braega shouted back, angrily. 'A story to frighten children, like the dog heads!'

The apparition shook its head and sighed. 'My son has travelled too long in a foreign land and has forgotten the lessons of his people.' Then his father turned to the log and laid his hands upon it. Fresh wood chips dropped away as his father's hands slowly squeezed, as though he were shaping wet clay rather than jagged wood. 'The dog-headed people were a chimeric race, part man and part wolf, sacred guardians of our people and fellow worshippers of the Goddess. They gave birth to the oracles, thinking their children would be friends to man. But man was fearful and rejected the gift of knowledge the oracles offered. Man made war upon the dog heads and their children, destroying almost all. Only a few remain.'

Now a pile of wood chips lay on the ground while the apparition held the product of his labours hidden inside his fists as he turned back to Braega. 'After the war, man claimed all the land as his own and, fearing he might abuse the oracles' power, the last dog heads gathered up the bones of their children and hid away. And in their absence many men forgot the Goddess. A great king rose up and murdered the old tribes, and the last memory of the dog heads died with them. Only the youngest children survived, adopted into the King's armies as lifelong soldiers: warrior slaves who forgot their former lives.'

Now the apparition opened its hands. Resting there Braega saw a beautifully carved figure, strong, long-limbed and graceful like the naked competitors at the Games. But, unlike them its beauty ended at the shoulders, for atop the figure was not the noble visage of a hero but the vulpine, atavistic head of a wolf. The contrast was so startling that Braega gasped as he looked upon it.

'You must find a shaman of the Goddess,' the apparition instructed, its voice growing distant. 'You must beg to see the head of the oracle of death, for with it you can know your destiny, Braega. You can know your fate… you can change it!'

The carving was gone and the pile of wood chips, too, and the chisel felt heavier in his hand, its handle thickening into the familiar hilt of a sword. Braega looked up in panic to see his father's face once more, perhaps for the last time in eternity. But already the apparition was fading away even as his father called out to him one last time. 'Remember your people, Braega. Remember who you are…'

Braega opened his eyes. Above him a violet moon rose over the whispering trees as a midnight breeze stirred their spindly branches. The moon: so beautiful, so magnificent, a goddess in her own right; worshipped by his people, guardian of their souls; she who took human form to walk among them and give them guidance, comfort and love. He drank in her beauty with his eyes and gratefully drew her sweet, cool breath into his lungs. He closed his eyes and felt at peace, his body cushioned in the thick green grass, the night breeze caressing his battle-scarred flesh like the soft touch of a lover's fingers.

Then he opened his eyes and saw the Goddess. She knelt above him, straddling his hips, and the soft night breeze which caressed his naked body was the silky waterfall of her jet black hair. It cascaded over him as she leant closer, until their lips touched and he felt the warmth of her, felt the rapid rise and fall of her breasts as their bodies responded to each other. The Goddess had answered the prayers of this lost, lonely son of the forest tribe, the last of his people; she had heard his cry and had come down from her high place to grant his wish and be his companion.

As they embraced, the moon was fractured by broken cloud that gusted across its face. The clouds traced shadows across the glade which threatened to block out the Goddess's divine light and plunge them both into darkness. He reached for her, afraid that she would be spirited away by the shade, that he would lose her and lose his last chance at happiness. But thankfully his hands closed on warm, pliant flesh and he clasped her to him, stroking her silky hair. Then he turned his face to hers, to gaze into her haunting eyes as the last light of the moon was blotted out, eyes that were tinged with blue behind deep black pupils in an ash grey face.

With an incoherent cry, he pushed her away and scrambled backwards through the slick grass. But Starling followed, stalking him on all fours, her eyes fixed on him, hands reaching for him, entreating him to stay. 'Please, Braega,' she begged, her voice husky with desire. 'Stay. Stay with me! Worship with me! The moon has a power to transform. As the moon grows stronger, so the transformation is more complete. Stay with me, Braega, and beneath the full moon I will give you what you want... what we both want!'

But his wits were gone and he did not heed her words. Finding his feet at last, he turned from her, from the half-human, half woman, half wolf. Half mad with loneliness and grief, she howled her pain as he fled, naked, into the night.

***

Wood chips fell like the tears of the forest onto the dirt floor. Starling blinked her eyes in the morning glare from the open door and looked across the hut at the man's broad back as he knelt beside the fire. He was clothed once more in his tunic and belt, but his skirt of mail lay discarded in the corner. The cooking pot bubbled gently and the smell of warm stew filled her nostrils. As she watched, Braega's arm moved as though he were stropping a blade on leather and more wood chips fell between his feet.

'Good morning,' she said, uncertainly.

He glanced back over his shoulder. 'Good morning,' he replied as he reached down and scooped the pile of chips into the fire. The sweet, scented smell of pine filled the cottage as they burned.

Starling swung her legs off the low cot, gathering the thin blanket around her nakedness. She had no memory of going to bed, just a chaotic jumble of images: rolling in the grass, screaming at the moon, running back to her cottage and smashing her pots in a frenzy – the fragments now lay in a swept heap by the door – fumbling under the cot for the stoppered jar and pouring its contents down her throat. And more than once, too, as the pounding behind her eyes testified.

Huddled in the blanket, she walked unsteadily across to the fire and sat down on the stool. 'Oh!' she said, suddenly.

'I made you a new one,' Braega explained.

She looked at him but he kept his eyes low. 'You were busy, last night,' she said.

'I found a fallen tree,' he began. 'One of the roots was the right shape, the right size. It is the way of my people to find what they need in the forest.'

'It was,' she agreed and noticed how he caught his breath at her past tense. She gazed into the fire a moment before turning her piercing white eyes back on him. 'Tell me, warrior of the forest tribe, why did you come back?'

He drew a shuddering breath. 'To pay a debt, if I can.'

'To your people? To your father?'

'No, to you.'

Starling sat back, puzzled. 'To me? What do you owe me?'

'I have wronged you,' Braega said, looking upon her for the first time without fear, suppressing the flicker of hesitation as his eyes met her visage. 'I attacked a holy shaman. I defiled your home with my blood. I cursed you and your kind and I dishonoured you by refusing your offer.' He turned to her and fell to his knee, his carving hidden in clasped hands. 'My people worshipped the Goddess and revered the dog heads as Her prophets. But I have travelled too long in the King's realm. There is much I have forgotten.' He hung his head. 'I thought you a monster and intended to kill you like an animal. I owe restitution.'

Starling was taken aback. 'And how will you pay your debt?' she asked, eventually.

'I will stay with you, as you bade me. I will remain as your companion or as your slave, as you will it. I will honour you and your people for the rest of my days.'

The fire crackled and spat. The warm stew bubbled gently. The golden sunlight played across the burning blue tattoos that ran across the taut, powerful curves of Braega's arms as Starling considered his offer. He would give himself to her and, if he was sincere, then according to the laws of his people, he would be bound by his word for all his years, or the Goddess would abandon his soul and leave it to wander the land in anguish. He would be her companion and her small home would no longer be a shrine to her loneliness but filled with the warmth and life of another. Each full moon she would worship not in somber isolation, but in ecstasy, as the Goddess intended. And, afterwards, she would not huddle alone on her narrow cot, tortured by dreams of intimacy, but would be warmed by the embrace of those strong arms… however reluctantly.

Slowly, she reached out with a long-nailed hand and gently touched his bowed head. She felt him shiver as she did so, but with revulsion at her touch, or fear of her answer?

But, oh! She had been alone for so long! Surely the Goddess would forgive her for taking a reluctant lover? He had been a willing slave to the murderous King all these years. Why not now a slave to love, instead? Surely the Goddess, who could see into the heart and soul of Her people, would forgive her this one selfish desire?

'Braega,' she began, her voice trembling. 'What is your heart's desire?'

He did not look up. 'To rejoin my people.'

'But your people are all dead.'

He nodded once beneath her hand and it was all she could do to contain her sob of pain as she read the anguish of his soul.

'Then I will grant you your heart's desire,' she said with a catch in her throat, 'even at the cost of mine.' He looked up now, but she had stood and turned away. She stooped to the dusty floor and retrieved something from among the sweepings by the door, then returned to the fire and offered it to Braega.

He looked at it, then up at her and found her terrible, piercing eyes moist with tears. Human tears. Reaching up, he took her offering as he held out his other hand, palm open. Resting there Starling saw a beautifully carved female figure with round breasts and a firm belly: strong, long-limbed and graceful. The Goddess of the moon. The face of the Goddess held wisdom, beauty and serenity. She seemed alive, so skilfully had Braega carved her, yet above this perfect vision was a wolf's head worn as a headdress. But not some dead thing was this: the animal's visage was noble, loyal and proud. And familiar. Starling saw that it was her, as she truly was. Braega had captured in the living wood Starling's true, secret self-image.

She accepted his offering as tears of grief and gratitude clouded her vision, so that she was spared the sight of the broken blade of her bronze sword plunging into his heart.

***

There were voices outside, coming closer. They were arguing.

'We shouldn't... this is holy ground.'

'Ay, there is old magic here.'

'Bite your tongues! You're not barbarians, you're King's men!'

'But they say she's a witch.'

'Ay, and that she's stronger than ten men!'

'They say she eats people!'

'Eats people? By the gods, you'll believe anything. Morons.'

Starling ignored them. Sitting before the fire on her new stool, she took up her mixing bowl. Along with her cooking pot it was all that had survived her drunken fury of the night before. There was still a residue of her elixir inside and she wiped a finger around the rim and sucked it, appreciatively. Then she hefted the bowl and, gripping the rim firmly, broke off a section of pot. Cracks spidered across the surface as she continued, working feverishly now to destroy the bowl. As the pieces crumbled to the floor, something began to emerge. Something chalky white and smooth, with strange contours. At last, when the last piece of pottery had fallen away, Starling held up her hands and stared into the empty eye sockets of a human skull.

The door to Starling's cottage rattled under three rapid blows. 'In the name of the King...' came the loudest voice.

'We seek one called Braega, formerly King's man and now condemned, as are all who shelter him from the King's justice!' Almost in the same moment the door was kicked open by a leather-booted foot and the bulky silhouette of a man in armour eclipsed the sun.

Starling raised her hooded head as though to regard the Guardsman. She had not moved from her stool, which she straddled, inelegantly, before the fire. The Guardsman came no further, halting at the threshold, his short spear held rigidly before him as though to ward off a wild animal. His eyes were fixed on the skull. As she watched, his gaze shifted, first to the soldier's skirt of mail that lay, apparently discarded, on the floor, then to the Guardsman's sword propped in the corner and, lastly, to the bubbling cooking pot before finally returning to the skull, and to her. Within the black depths of her hood Starling drew back her lips to expose her wet, toothy smile.

He fled.

As the sound of many running feet diminished into the distance, Starling picked up Braega's carved figurine and gazed at it. Then she upended the skull, placed the carving within and raised the head of Death, the last and most powerful of the oracles, raised it and stared intently into orbits. Beyond the open doorway of her hut the afternoon sun bathed the forest glade in golden light. A gentle breeze stroked the dense bracken, briefly exposing a patch of disturbed ground where a human figure lay, wrapped in a shroud, peacefully awaiting nightfall and the coming of the moon. But it didn't matter. Starling knew that few things the living did really mattered, for the soul was already long gone. Gone to a happier place, far away in time and memory.

And through the eyes of Death, Starling watched and smiled while, under his father's careful guidance, the boy that was Braega cut his first simple carving from a forest log.

Three Conversations or How I Burned your Mother

By Matt Beeson

These words herein were found, handwritten in script, on a sheaf of papers tied together loosely with some old twine. The circumstances of their finding I shall here describe, yet first I feel the words themselves must be set to print for all to read as a warning to the hubris of man in his dealings with the occult or his dealings with the other sex. I hope my humble translation of the cursive will be straightforward enough to read and understand, for be prepared, reader: the culmination of events is not for the meek or faint-hearted. It reeks of a witchcraft so villainous, subtle and cunning that many would not even notice it as it pervaded their daily existence: a witchcraft so commonplace that one may find it in any low tavern or high house of this fair land of England.

Note you that the author of this text speaks himself in the first person, as if to tell a story of his own personal happenings. Know you, also, that the scene which I – in my haphazard style and lowly function as narrator of the piece – shall attempt to describe for you upon your completion of the passages, which leaves me yet with a shiver at the recollection, I do believe to be clear confirmation of the truth of these writings, as our author saw it, the truth before our God, and the truth before the object of his affection, to whom he writes.

Enough of my preamble. The writings are entitled: 'On the three discussions that bore you thus, my darling' and they begin like this…

***

A Meeting with your Mother

I rode through the night, I remember that. By the time I arrived at Weatherford-on-Sand there was a glow on the horizon and Shakespeare was all but lame. We pulled up at the edge of the village, I dismounted and nodded a greeting to a fellow on his way to the fields. I remember him because he would suffer me no acknowledgement in return save a gawking review up and down of my person before he ambled gracelessly upon his way. I led the bard through the village, which was poor by my recollection, but no more so than any other I had passed in the West Riding; there was little charm.

I shall not tarry too long in descriptions of the place, save to say that your mother's house was quite different and yet the same. It was not out of place in these surrounds and yet it had an odd appeal. It was neat and cared for. Blooms lay in baskets around the windows and by the gate that opened to a short path. I tied Shakespeare to a post of the fence or a tree or some such upright. I fed him some oats or an apple from my pocket, which he accepted with a whicker. He was then yet a good horse with several more years left in him.

As I opened the gate, I noticed a small yet significant collection of wooden crucifixes and other symbols of the

Faith, piled discreetly behind the fence, which I think I bent to inspect briefly. At the end of the path there was a green door, adorned by a wreath of coriander. The smell was pungent, fresh and glorious; I can remember it now as if I lay again in a bath of the stuff. I raised my left hand to hammer on the wood and reached the right into my breast for my bible. I remember quite vividly the lightning stab of fear and shock when my hand felt nought but empty cloth, my most critical crutch distinguished by absence. Mildly frantic, I cast about. After some panicked moments I spied the tome sat atop the pile by the gate with the other Godly things. It must have slipped from my pocket straight onto the pile.

I had set off back down the path to retrieve the Book when I heard the door open behind me. I remember being quite startled. Startled. A descriptive word. Not a single start but a series of starts, the frequentative suffix never more appropriate. The first start came at the sound of the door, the second at the sight of your mother's face, which was by far the most beautiful I had ever seen, the third from my uncontrolled wheeling and stumbling into her arms, the fourth from the scent of coriander and rosemary that flooded from her bosom – within which my face was now solidly embedded – and, finally, the fifth start from her voice.

Her voice. Perhaps the years that have passed since have added a more complex flavour to my memories, embellished and coloured them with hues of purple and gold, but I remember her voice was more music than words. It lilted and sang, a flute that carried the words on a gentle breeze to my ears.

"Hello," she said. "Are you quite comfortable?"

I reared back, the last of my dignity evanescent in the morning sunlight.

"Wah, ahh, damn, I'm gabbling," I gabbled, or something

equally uninspiring to that effect or otherwise. With a burn to my cheeks, I felt a modicum of composure raise itself from my sandbags to my voice box and I tried again.

"Madam," I said, mustering all the gravitas my trampled esteem had to offer, which, if it could have been measured, would not have registered on any but the finest of scales. "Madam, I would speak with you on a matter of great import." To top it all, my voice gave a squeak as it caught on the 'gr' of great and I was forced to cough drily, which brought tears to my eyes.

She gave me a look up and down, in a manner not dissimilar to the fellow at the village boundary, yet with a somewhat greater demeanour. She saw me quite clearly, for all my pomposity and regimental finery, moist eyes and all, a naked wretch, exposed in my endeavours, on the porch of a lady whom I had come to brand as a witch.

"Well," she said. "You'd better come in then," and your mother led me inside.

***

I shall attempt to render the details of my conversation with your mother accurately and in an impartial fashion. Yet I know the thirteen and some years that have passed since have altered my recollection, likely to offset the shudders of a life ill-lived and make it seem to myself in my quiet moments that I was less of an ass than indeed I was. I do remember that I had barely set foot across the threshold when a torrent of verbal effluent flooded forth, as if all the eastside sluice gates had been released at once upon the virgin Thames.

***

"Madam, you are hereby charged with crimes of witchery. The Shire-folk hereabouts have sent a missive to the Lord Commander, Protector of the Western Watch, to describe to him in his capacity as commander-in-chief of the Legion of Watchers, a series of heinous acts perpetrated by yourself against the good and natural personages of those who would live GODLY lives: INNOCENT lives free from your UNGodly pollution. I have come to exorcise you so far as I, a humble Watcher, can hope to do so, to rid you of the demons that coarse through your fetid veins. I charge you by this holy book…" Again I reached inside my breast only to rediscover the truancy of my desired prop. "…damnit to hell! By MY holy book and all the holy images of our Lord and Saviour upon which it currently resides, I charge you. With all good conscience… what are you doing?"

✳✳✳

During the time in which I had set sail upon the frothing sea of my ill-judged rant, slavering tongue flapping into waving motion on this ocean of viscous drivel, the seeming object of my ire had made her way to the small kitchen area of her humble home and was set about placing a pot of water atop a cold stove.

"I'm making tea," she said matter-of-factly.

"Tea?" I inquired.

"Tea," she replied. "If you'll be staying, we'll be needing tea."

"Tea," I repeated. I let the word linger. "You understand, Madam that I am here to charge you with the crime of being a witch? This is no time for fripperies and trivialities. What do you say in your defence?"

"Well, so far, whilst you have rambled at some length, you

haven't actually accused me of anything at all." She lit the stove, and then turned to face me. I remember fireflies dancing in her eyes. "Do you perhaps have a list of actual crimes I am alleged to have committed, against which I might more reasonably hope to make a defence?"

I stepped further into the house, through a small living area, to set my satchel on a humble oaken dining table. I opened it and withdrew the scroll. I weighed the paper in my hand as a thought occurred to me.

"You are dressed," I said directly, to which she merely raised an eyebrow. To my shame I remember that I became a little heated. "That is to say, you are fully dressed and made ready, and the curtains are drawn. Yet the day is still very new, not to mention that you greeted me at the door, before I had even knocked upon it."

"Your powers of observation are truly impressive." I remember not a trace of mockery in her voice and her smile had been gentle, yet I felt warmth rise in me again.

"You knew of my visit in advance of my coming." I made an accusatory gesture: the official scroll of the Western Watch was wagged at her; the roll of vellum upon which was written the list of charges became a metaphor for itself. The irony was lost upon me at the time.

"I assure you, sir, that I did not. I had intended to take a walk to the Mushroom Wood and was on my way there when I came across you thrashing at my threshold. You and your scroll have already cost me the best of the morning." Her tone was still pleasant but there was a sharp edge now that set my face tingling.

I consciously reigned myself back. I had never quite been sure whether I believed in witchery or not. I suppose that's an odd thing for a career Witcherman to say, but there we were. I decided to err on the side of caution, as Cervantes would have it, to be 'slower of tongue and quicker of eye.' Besides, should the trial go against this woman, I was now about to begin the process of condemning her to a painful death. Better kindness first and place faith in God's grace for my ultimate redemption. She seemed to sense a change in the air.

"You'd better get on with it, then," she said, turning back to the preparation of leaves and water.

"I'm sorry." And I meant it, peculiarly. I was peaceful, more in control of myself than I had felt in a long time, maybe ever, certainly more than I had felt since tying Shakespeare to the fence. The window was now to my immediate right; I stole a glance at the old chap stood patiently waiting, enjoying the sun.

"Well, I suppose it can't be helped."

"You did seem unsurprised by my arrival."

She sighed wearily, her tea now brewing. She turned back towards me: "There's little to surprise a woman of imagination."

As I pondered this retort, she invited me to sit at the table with a small gesture; I obliged, noting that I was more than a little weary myself. We sat down and I felt myself staring at her. I don't know if she was more beautiful then or now where she lives only in my memories, but I had never seen anyone or anything, before or since, in which I found such wonder. She had actual tresses: auburn and cascading down to the breast with which I was already altogether too intimately acquainted for any honest pretence at decorum. Hazel eyes. Witch hazel.

With that intrusive thought of random association, I came to myself again. I don't know how long I had stared at her then, but now it was your mother's turn to blush slightly. Yet she did not turn away or make any affected plea to coy shyness. She simply regarded me patiently.

Gently, I opened the scroll, breaking the Lord Commander's seal. Flakes of vermillion wax distributed themselves across the oaken surface, and formed motes in the sunlight. I began to read: "Helen Fosse, Witch." How little pretence there was, with no sense of the potential for innocence. Witch presumptive. I think she grimaced; maybe that was me. "By the duty and privilege vested in the Lord Commander's proud..."

"I think you can skip the pleasantries and get straight to the nub of it." She laid her hands on the table. There was dirt beneath her fingernails.

"Yes." My eyes rolled down to the list of charges. "On 14th July, in the year of our Lord 1701, you did make well the child of Mary-Anne Postlethwaite, one Clarabelle Postlethwaite, from a bout of dysentery, with strange herbs and incantations."

Her eyes rolled up to the beams. "The girl had the shits and I gave her some herbal tea. She had lost nearly all her water, poor love. The *incantations* were my soothing her while the stomach cramps..." She must have seen an expression on my face that I had not consciously willed into being and waved me to carry on.

"On 3rd March, 1702, you did minister the birth of Councillor William Eccles's first born son, Michael James Eccles, and in so doing did cause his lady wife, Sarah Eccles, to bleed and die."

Your mother's jaw was set and her hazel eyes were moistening, I noted.

"Do you want me to continue?" I asked, as gently as I could.

"Well, you came all this way." She glanced out of the window, so the sun caught her eyes, then wiped across them with the back of her hand, before replacing it next to the other on the table. Palms down and dry-eyed she looked back to me. "It would be a shame for you to stop so soon."

It was my turn to grimace; a shiver ran through me. I forced my way through the rest of the charges, some twenty-three instances over a period of six years. By the end, she seemed sad, but certainly unbowed.

"How do you answer these charges?" I asked.

"How do you answer them?" she challenged. I opened my mouth to respond, but she continued, and I waited for a few seconds like one of the Commander's carp before accepting defeat. "I see no charges here, only the exaggerated and embellished claims of folk who are variously ungrateful and ignorant. Who has done the embellishing: the folk or the fuckers who would have me burned on their account? Sometimes the poor and the ignorant feel they do their duty to their god. And there is always someone ready to take their innocence and make some nefarious profit from it. They would have people such as me blamed for the ills they will not address lest it cost them a gold plate or three. So, I ask you. How do *you* answer these charges?'

There was more of it, but that is what I remember; throughout the whole speech her palms stayed flat on the table, as if in some kind of assurance that she meant me no harm. To be frank with you, my darling, were it not for the rapier I habitually kept slung against my left hip and the dirk then jiggering my right – the former of which I still fancy I had some modest level of skill with – I would not have felt comfortable that I could have fended off your mother should she *have* intended me harm, either physical or magical.

I pondered her accusation. Even as I was then, a Witcherman of probity, if not conviction, I struggled to pluck from the charges anything that amounted to more than misadventure. With most, as in the primary case of the Postlethwaites, I could discover no moral wrong, let alone a crime. She clearly had learning and a willingness to apply it; she was no shy flower. She was also quite lovely, and was either yet to take a husband or had already taken one or more who, for whatever reason, could not stay. I began to mentally chip away at the reports on the scroll, to reimagine them in context, to see the ignorant peasants who saw magic in medicine, the jealous and spiteful women who saw the twinkling fancies of their wandering husbands...

I bowed my head a little, then raised my eyes slightly to regard her from beneath my brow, which was by then quite furrowed.

"I cannot," I answered at last. "I see nothing in this scroll for which you should be given the lash, let alone the pyre." I stood to leave.

"Wait," she interjected. "You haven't even sipped your tea." She rose and gestured for me to sit. I took a few seconds to acquiesce, neither sat nor fully stood, by which time she was returning from the stove with a steaming pot and cups, glancing at me and smiling briefly. "Shall I be mother?" she inquired, pouring my tea.

***

Shakespeare and I left the village of Weatherford-on-Sand a number (I have little inkling to the exact count) of happy days later. The light was strangely more fine and the road more certain. My mind and senses were full of your mother, her singing voice so firm and sure, her hazel eyes that seared deep into me, welding the pieces of my fractured soul. Hot baths infused with piquant coriander still stinging my skin was melancholic pleasantness; the sensations faded slowly with the light as we rode into the waxing dusk.

***

A Meeting with the Commander

I would like to report to you that I was stood serenely gazing out of the large window – that was the style of the day – with my hands clasped behind my back in classic pose when the Lord Commander came to greet me after my extended wait of some forty minutes. Yet I fear I had begun to pace, as is my wont.

The great doors opened, and he stalked across the landing from his rooms. This was not the first time I had met with him, yet as always I could not help but remark – to my own self for I would not dare to think such aloud – how unimpressive was his personage for one so seemingly exalted. His diminutive stature made the required degree of fawning all the more difficult to accomplish believably. Yet, again as always, I found a way to manage it.

He approached and, when some six feet or so away, threw to me what he had been carrying, which I came to see was a thick leather tabard. I caught it – fortunately, as I was not prepared – and looked down at the smaller man quizzically.

"You fancy yourself as a swordsman, I understand," he growled. "Put it on."

I hesitated for a second, but his drawing his rapier and adopting the stance hastened me to fumbling action. I noticed that the tabard the Lord was already wearing was fitted out with leather plastrons and, as I clumsily entered mine, pulling the stiff straps through the buckles, I noticed that mine was not. My own blade was barely unsheathed when he advanced with purpose, his first wild slash coming contemporaneously with a call of 'En-garde.'

Despite my lack of readiness, I parried his initial advance easily. Flicking my wrist, I deposited his blade at an uncomfortable angle to his right. My ensuing lunge in riposte was instinctive, scoring the point easily upon his protected midriff.

"Touché!" he called, although there could have been no

doubt. We formed up again, and this time he made more of a duel of the exchange than I had been expecting. I was forced back to the bannister, upon which I gave my left elbow an ungainly rap. The Commander used the moment to score at my shoulder; I felt even then that, but for his poor aim, my exposed underarm would have been cut. For the first time, I considered the possibility that, for some reason or other, my tiny master was trying to do me actual bodily injury.

We took our stances after a moment's brush down. I steeled myself and took on a certain intensity of concentration. The duel of this next round was vicious, with more than a hint of corps-à-corps. It ended as he tripped and stumbled to a knee, and I held my tip above his chest with a flourish. Noticing the man seemed winded, I paused. He held up his sword hand to request a pause for breath. Thus distracted, I saw his move too late. He took up his rapier swiftly with his off hand and struck up at my exposed underarm. The pain shot through me and I dropped my sword. Blood, MY blood, spattered and then continued to drip onto the polished oak. The Commander's smile was sardonic.

He stood and offered his hand then shook his head in amusement when I took it. He snapped his fingers and a servant who had been waiting hitherto unseen came scurrying over. We adjourned to a corner of the landing in which was provided an arrangement of sofas and chairs. We sat facing one another, his manservant on my right tending to my wounded wing. It was then that I finally caught a glimpse of the Commander's motives.

"She had you, didn't she, boy? Don't answer, it's written plain as day all over your face. You let her under your guard and she had you. And now you're here to convince me that she shouldn't burn. Well I tell you, lad, I don't give two ounces of shit for what you came here to say. You have a duty to perform and when Cuthbert…" or whatever his name was, I'm damned if I can remember "…has finished bandaging your ego then off you fuck to perform it."

I was taken aback by the harshness of his words. I had hitherto considered myself to be something of a favourite of the Commander, your grandfather and he being as close as they were. Yet he had just cut me with both his words and his actual sword. I was aggrieved and this grievance gave me something of a stomach, at least temporarily. I expounded at length upon your Mother's many virtues and the assured nature of her innocence. There was much repetition and embellishment, but the crux I shall attempt to record.

"She is a woman of knowledge and learning. She has nothing but good will towards the townsfolk, and any folk for that matter. The claims against her are undoubtedly false, trumped up by jealous women or threatened men. They would have us believe that she has used some sort of unholy art, yet all she has done is apply the learning of four generations of womenfolk in her line for the advantage of those who come upon hardship or trials. She offers succour where no other can and she is repaid with ignorance and accusation. What's more, we pay heed to this ridiculous accusation. Or, maybe worse? Maybe we foment this accusation, encourage it, build upon it and then try and burn her for it. Is that what we are?"

The Commander finally held up his hand to silence me. The words that followed, I am ashamed to convey, I remember with great clarity.

"You are not a man of God, are you, lad?" I began to protest but his hand balled to a fist and I refrained. "Your father was none either, and nor am I. Of course we can play the part when we need to, but we are men of worldly things, of necessity and action. Or, perhaps, I have misjudged you? Perhaps your proclivity for the words and undoubted talent for the plays has given air to your thoughts and imaginings and *philosophies*." He laid an emphasis here that showed in exactly what low esteem he held such dalliances as thought and philosophy. "There is no place for empathy and compassion in our line of work. They are indeed the tools of the devil."

He smiled again, perhaps impressed by his command of irony, and paused as if to let me speak, but by then I had already said more than I should. I was sullen and contemplating either an exit or an attempt upon his life with my weaker arm. I duly settled upon neither. That may have been my most fatal decision. Seeing I was seemingly mute, the Commander continued on another tack.

"The duty you hold is not to me, nor to the Legion. Your duty is to this Kingdom, or Queendom, or whatever. This England. We are held together as a people by a strong fabric, a stuff of meat and sinew. Yet we must not slacken. Even the strongest of blades can be broken by a keener cut, even the thickest of walls can be breached by a cunning engine..." The metaphors and euphemisms cascaded and tumbled then like a... never mind. Eventually they came to an end. "She has bewitched you, be sure of that. You have been hexed by her wiles and charms. You have forgotten your duty because of her..." He spoke a word I cannot record for you, my darling.

Incensed, I stood to challenge him, wounded arm and all. He rose to meet me, eye to chin for a moment of momentum. His was the greater. A hand on my sternum seated me again as quickly as if I was nought but rump. His diminutive height took nothing away from the imposing manner in which he towered over me then.

"We all have our part to play. We are united in our hatred of the Frenchman, for example; to assure us in that we have Godolphin and Marlborough. We have the black man and the Chinaman and the nonce, but they are not our concern; the proponents of their hatred need so little encouragement that the fire of their ire is as close to self-sustaining as we could ever wish; yet their quarries are too few. You and I, the Witchermen: our part is to remind the *innocent* folk of our good nation who they are, and whom they are not. Make no mistake: the Witch has her, or his…" we were always keen to avoid any potential for insinuation of discrimination on the part of the Legion, and yet I only ever recall us burning witches of the female variety "…part to play in this grand fabric. The Witch's part is to burn. She must be set to flame as a symbol of our unity against the unholy."

He leaned over me then, taking the scruff of my cape into his tiny hands. I remember that I recoiled at the stench of his unwashed mouth.

"Our duty is to make sure that happens," he spat. "If we fail in our duty, and if these ideas of women gain hold in the minds of the commonfolk, then this fabric is rent." He tore my cape, which I do confess I had been at least half expecting, yet my pride and energy for redress had sunk again to a low-point from which I fear I did not fully recover. Pausing for a moment, apparently to allow the full weight of his dramatic gesture to permeate my consciousness, he forged on.

"Think of what this will do to our Kingdom. Once the people can see that they do not need the Witchermen to protect them from the witches, once they see that they can think for themselves and learn for themselves, they will see that they do not need the protection of our Queens and Lords, our protectors of the realm. They will want an equal voice, a chance for *destiny*, to become persons of their own. This we cannot allow, for when this comes, we are done. Not just as Witchermen but as men of *destiny*, men of land. We will become equal to *them*."

The insight that built itself from the Commander's words

brought with it a momentary frisson. As I left the great house and mounted Shakespeare, who was waiting and groomed beyond the portcullis, I weighed his exposition. On the one hand there was your mother, the most beautiful and fragrant woman I had ever encountered, who was even then awaiting my return. On the other was the truth of our world and the necessities that came with that truth. I, aboard the bard, rode steadily into the setting sun, wounded in body and spirit. As my journey developed, so did my train of thought. My ambivalence never fully waned, yet somewhere along the rode I found a steel set that determined the course of action that led me at last to you.

***

A Meeting with You

And so, my darling, all that remains is for me to describe to you, in these pages, how you came to be and what became of your mother, whom you never knew. I cannot describe a conversation as such, as I have never found the courage to tell you more than the fact – which is more omission than truth – that your mother died in childbirth. You must be satisfied with a confession, for that is what this is.

I hope you will judge me kindly, perhaps on these last thirteen years when I have done my best to raise and love you, despite the terrible crimes I lay out for you here. I have loved you these years and done the best that a man could hope to do, but always in grief at the knowledge that I had already failed you before you were born. You may find this truth, or confession, difficult to bear and believe, but you must know it and, as much as I would dearly desire to, I cannot spare you the details. This consumption that has wracked me for the last years will soon come to mortal fruition, and with perhaps my greatest regret, I must soon leave you for the last time.

I returned to your mother some days after my visit to the Commander, but I did not return alone. Instead, I came with a force of Watchers at my back. There was no anger in your mother's eyes as she greeted me, only distance and sadness. We led her to the square and made a show of her trial. Never once did she speak in her defence, even as the assembled masses bayed as one, hungry for, I truly believe, they knew not what.

Upon conclusion, I pronounced to the crowd, in my delegated duty as Captain of the Watch, that your mother was guilty of witchcraft. They roared in celebration; the chants to hasten her fate began. The pyre was already prepared, piles of tinder and thicker logs for a lasting cook. Cruciform symbols, crudely hewn from chunks of wood and tied together with leather strapping, were leaned against the base. We tied her securely to the central mast. The innocent folk of Weatherford-on-Sand pelted her then with whatever vegetable matter they could find, as was the tradition. I retreated a sufficient distance to escape much of the splatter.

Another of the Watchers handed me a lit torch. I regarded your mother and she looked back at me. The sadness remained, and there was also pity. Even then there was a voice in my head telling me that I could effect some sort of daring rescue, draw my sword, untie my beloved with a deft slash or two, and cut our way free of the mob. Yet this voice was drowned by the words of the Commander: 'They will want an equal voice, a chance for *destiny*, to become persons of their own.' Besides, my sword arm was still bandaged and weak.

I mistook my intruding confusion for a charlatan sent to thwart my purpose; instead of giving due pause it only served to strengthen my steel. I lit the pyre myself. Only then did I turn away from your mother's gaze. The mob grew quiet in some kind of gruesome awe and I heard the crackle as the flames licked up. I heard nought else then, not so much as a bird chirruping. No screams or sounds of any kind came from your mother. I looked back to her and saw that her eyes were now closed; death was already upon her, long before the flames had fully begun their work. Later, I speculated that it may have been shock, or perhaps she had ministered to herself some of her own magic in advance of my coming. That she had always known when and how to expect me.

My steel intent soon gave way to a dreamlike state. The heat of the inferno was immense. The others had backed away as the flames caught but I could not. Perhaps that explains why it was to my ears that your cries came and not to the others. I saw you then, born from your mother in the flames, her last act bringing life from death. I suffered painful burns as I leapt forward to pull you from the fire, but I knew that I must and I did not hesitate; your mother's part was not yours. With the assured certainty that you were my child girding my resolve, I rescued you before the flames could take you from me as well. As I cradled you in my damaged arms, bandages partly burned away, oblivious to the pain, I gazed into your eyes for the first time and knew that I would love and care for you for the rest of my life. As the pyre took away the last of your mother, we left the square together, accompanied by the astonished stares of the Watchers and onlookers, and the faintest hint of coriander in the smoke that drifted on the breeze.

I resigned my commission in the Legion immediately thereafter. Your grandfather was vociferous in his objection; the terrible names he called you I shall not repeat. Our circumstances have been modest since and I have always regretted not being able to provide you with a life befitting the debt I owe.

You are here now as I write, having come to visit me in my

sickbed, as you are so good to do, before I sleep. You look so pretty, like your mother, in that lace dress and the yellow floral bonnet. I know we could not afford the finest and you must wear the same from day to day, yet we have always survived and been happy. We are supported by our love for each other, not finance and fineries.

I write these final words before I sleep as you lay a kiss upon my brow. When I have finished, I will tie together these pages in a package for you to find when you come to wake me of the morning. I am sure that you will not succeed. With all my sins packaged thus, I shall go to dream of a life that never was, in a world that could never be, we three together, ever loved and ever free.

✳✳✳

So then it comes to my part in this. The writing I have conveyed to you must be set within a context, a description for the circumstances of the finding recounted. It was the stench that led me there, off the road to the hovel in the woods, in the hope of doing some good or claiming some reward. There had been some attempt to keep the house in a mode fit for habitation, yet the repairs were clumsy and not the work of a skilled craftsman. Inside the gate near the outer wall lay an old pile of bones, which may have been a horse, flesh gnawed clean from them.

The smell came from the corpse of the man whom I presume to have been the author of the work, for he still clutched two things, one of which was this sheaf of papers, tied together in twine. The other I shall come to. I do not know what possessed me to take the papers away with me, but take them away I did, for the queerness of the surroundings compelled me to leave, as did the foetid reek of what remained of the man, who had quite clearly to me then died in great suffering, bewitched by something to which at that point I could not put a name.

Upon reading the papers later at relative leisure, I learned the nature of the bewitchment. I speak to you from no meagre experience, for I have been a victim as much as a perpetrator of this, the kind of witchcraft that besets all folk too weak and trivial to resist. This witchcraft of charisma and guile is wielded by those who would bend our minds against others who are different. Not that there can ever be ascribed a lack of virtue inherent to the difference; more that the difference offers an opportunity for strength and coalescence for those of us who lack it. Where I have found joy and solace in the vilification of men who would lie happily with other men, I too have been subjected to the hurling of bile and vitriol to press me to atone for no other crime than the blackness of my skin. There have always been and always will be those dark-blooded minds that speak of *Others*, and hate, and necessity, and justification of egregious action against the innocent personages who are blameless in all except the blame that is inherent in their *Otherness*.

I entreated you at the outset to trust in me as to the truth of these happenings, though hitherto I acknowledge that I have provided very little basis for that trust, and I shall redress this shortly. You have read of proclaimed grief and sadness, regret for crimes inflicted. Yet you would be forgiven for an interpretation of these writings as light words only, self-justification, and post hoc rationalisation. The writings here are all and none of those things.

I found our author lying upon a dirty bed, surrounded by more gnawed bones and bloody rags. On his rotting forehead I could make out a smudge of ash, which at first I thought odd until I further inspected. In his arms, as I have mentioned, rested two things. The first, the papers, the contents of which you have since digested. The second was a burned and blackened cruciform faggot, crudely hewn and tied together with charred leather strapping. This cross was wrapped in tattered and ragged cloth that may have once passed for a lace dress, topped at the last with an old, yellow, floral bonnet.

***

Take this then as a warning, but also a gift. It is a reminder of what the mind of man or woman is capable of when it subjects itself to such terrible dissonance from which there can be no resolution, a permanent suspension that destroys the spirit and drives the mind to madness. For all the *witches* we each send silent to their lonely pyres, we gather together the remnant pieces of our souls in twine and charred leather strapping. For all the love that bears not fruit nor plants no seed, we heap lies upon lies upon desperate hope. But what is hope when truth is done? Naught but smoke and burning.

About the Authors

Nadine Dalton-West

Nadine Dalton-West is the author of BFS award-shortlisted 'The Women's Song' (in the *Fight Like a Girl* collection) and 'Rusalka' (in *The Book of Orm*), both published by Kristell Ink. She is learning to play the cello, and is happiest near animals or large bodies of water. She is on Twitter and Instagram as @ andiekarenina.

Adam Lively

Adam Lively has published four novels (*Blue Fruit* (1987), *The Burnt House* (1989), *The Snail* (1991) and *Sing the Body Electric* (1993)), short stories (his story 'Voyage' was included in *Best British Short Stories 2013* (Salt)) and non-fiction (including *Democracy in Britain: A Reader* (1994) and *Masks: Blackness, Race and the Imagination* (1998)). He currently lectures at Middlesex University. In addition to this writing and teaching, he has worked in the past as a Producer of TV and radio documentaries, and is a regular reviewer of contemporary fiction in the national press.

Isabella Hunter

When her parents were pulled into a meeting with her primary school teacher regarding the prevalent theme of death in her writing, they thought it was hilarious and encouraged her to keep writing what she loved. It is no surprise, then, that Isabella Hunter found herself included in The Horror Writers' Association Reading List of 2019. She has written for publishers including Kristell Ink, Iron Faerie, CultureCult, and others. Her writing is a mix of fantasy, horror, and folklore from around the world.

You can find her on both Facebook and Twitter under Isabella Hunter. Alternatively, her blog (isabellahunter.blog) has a full list of all publications and anything else she feels the need to write about.

A J Dalton

A J Dalton (the 'A' is for Adam) is an author of science fiction and fantasy. He has published twelve books to date, including *The Book of Orm*, *The Book of Angels*, and *The Book of Dragons* with Kristell Ink, the *Empire of the Saviours* trilogy with Gollancz, *I am a Small God* with Admanga Publishing, and *The Satanic in Science Fiction and Fantasy* with Luna Press Publishing. His website is www.ajdalton.eu, where there is much to entertain fans of SFF. He is to be found hanging out with his cat Cleopatra either in Manchester or London, init.

Garry Coulthard

Garry Coulthard is a writer based in the North-West of England who has a BA and MA in creative writing. He is rubbish at grammar. He often goes by the nickname Grim, which if you knew him in person you'd find odd as he's quite nice. Some of the things he writes about, however… Have a look on his website (www.grimgarry.com) or find him on Twitter (@GrimGarry).

Michael Conroy

Michael Conroy owns Sirius Editorial, an online literary journal featuring stories and essays by international writers. He also teaches English, and works as a freelance editor, proof-reader and copywriter. Fiction is a bad habit of his. Sniff him out at www.siriuseditorial.com. Or follow him on Facebook and Twitter (@siriuseditorial).

Michael Victor Bowman

Michael was once chased by an angry hippo in Tanzania, which was the most interesting seven seconds of his life. The most interesting six seconds are another story…

Michael grew up preferring fantasy to football. As a writer he'll try any genre at least once, but always comes home to science fiction and fantasy. His published works include 'The Lucky Ones' (in *The Book of Angels* collection), a story about angels trapped on Earth, and *Black and White*, a new take on the mythology of dragons. His books can be found on Amazon and, when he isn't writing, he can usually be found walking a dog.

If you liked 'Heart's Desire' please stop by to leave a comment because, as Charles Buxton said, silence is the severest criticism.

Facebook at www.facebook.com/michaelvictorbowman, Twitter at @mvictorbowman.

Sick of social media? Try this: www.michaelvictorbowman. com. It's an actual blog! It's easy on the eyes, has an enlightened comment policy, and good taste in books. Sounds like the ideal Tinder date…

Matt Beeson

Matt Beeson is father to Brandon, husband to Nola; these are the things he knows for certain. He works as an engineer and occasionally even does some engineering. He primarily writes reports and the occasional technical paper; *The Book of Witches* is his first foray into fiction and he very much hopes that it won't be his last. In his spare time he likes to read lots of things – his tastes are eclectic – while sitting, preferably. Sometimes just sitting will do. He was once a musician and hopes to be one again someday. Until then there is always chocolate and coffee. He is occasionally to be found on Twitter (@Phaeduck).

Acknowledgements

A whole slew of people have helped put together the *The Book of Witches*. I'd like to thank...

- Sammy HK Smith of Kristell Ink, whose tolerance and good faith are equally rare amongst publishers

- Charlotte Pang, who produced the gorgeous book cover

- Matt Beeson, Michael Victor Bowman, Michael Conroy, Garry Coulthard, Isabella Hunter and Adam Lively, my inspiring co-authors, who have contributed their work, hearts and minds in return for a small pile of groats

- Rob Clifford, who did his damnedest

- Mum and Dad, who continue to support the literary ambitions of their son against all good reason and common sense

- Nadine Dalton-West, my beautiful wife, whose only flaw is that she writes better than me

- all those fantasy fans who keep insisting it's all worth it

- and, as per the dedication, every woman or person who has suffered persecution or demonization for who they are!

I humbly salute you all!

A J Dalton

Also by A.J. Dalton

from Kristell Ink Publishing

The Book of Orm

This exciting new collection brings together the writing talents of international fantasy author A J Dalton, Nadine West (Bridport Anthology) and Matt White (prize-winning scriptwriter). Magic, myth and heroic mayhem combine in a world that is eerily familiar yet beautifully liberating.

The Book of Angels

Would you want to be an angel? The pay's terrible and you get nothing but complaints from dissatisfied mortals. This exciting new collection brings together the writing talents of international fantasy author A J Dalton, Matt White (prize-winning scriptwriter), Caimh McDonnell (writer for Mock the Week), Sammy HK Smith (friend to gods and demons), Andrew Coulthard (award-nominated short story writer) and Michael Bowman (widely worshipped by those who know about such things).

"Divine, divisive and downright dastardly!" – Carl Rhinebeck

The Book of Dragons

He saw dragons everywhere, and that was why they'd put him in a secure unit. They told him there was no such thing as dragons. But he'd seen unprovoked attacks on the street, violence break out in an apparently quiet bar, rage overtake people on crowded pavements, and supposed peace-keepers use shocking degrees of force. In such moments, the beasts revealed themselves. They could be glimpsed louring from beneath ridged brows, snarling in the corner of your eye and leering between your rapid and confused blinks. You had to be quick, mind, and know what to look for. But once you knew about them, it was somehow harder for them to convince you that you'd imagined what you'd seen, that you'd been mistaken, or that it had all been some trick of the light. Once you knew about them and properly believed in them, it seemed they had less power over you, less ability to blind you to them and less general impossibility. What really worried him, though, was whether they suspected he saw them. And if they began to suspect, what might they then do to him?

kristell-ink.com